Alas, She Drowned

A STRATFORD UPON AVONDALE MYSTERY
BOOK ONE

MONICA KNIGHTLEY

ISBN-13: 978-1542698344
ISBN-10: 1542698340

Also by Monica Knightley

The Stratford Upon Avondale Mysteries:

COME, BITTER POISON
O HAPPY DAGGER
'TIS THE WITCHING TIME

Paranormal Romances from Soul Mate Publishing:

THE VAMPIRE'S PASSION
MISS AUSTEN'S VAMPIRE

Writing as Monica Duddington:

BAND GEEKS AND RIPTIDES

(A Young Adult contemporary novel from Soul Mate Publishing)

To my family, with love

LAERTES:
Alas, then she is drowned.

GERTRUDE:
Drowned, drowned.

LAERTES:
Too much of water hast thou, poor Ophelia.

From *Hamlet*
By William Shakespeare

~ one ~

A S I PLACED THE SANDWICH board advertising, "Authentic English Cream Teas, $7.99", outside my twee tea room I came to a realization. In the past two weeks alone, I'd had all the murder, mayhem, scandal, and treachery I could handle.

When I'd moved from my home in Philadelphia to this small town four months earlier I had no idea it was such a hotbed of scandal. Murders were commonplace; duplicity abounded; treachery was to be expected.

And yet the place is bucolic beyond words. Nestled in a rural corner of a western state, it is surrounded by orchards and vineyards. But much of its claim to fame is the center of town which resembles a quaint English village, with every building seeming to have been lifted from Tudor or Victorian England. Mullioned windows, exposed timbers, bay windows, gables, and jettied top floors appear to be building code requirements.

1

But still, all that murder and duplicity.

Murder and duplicity that could be found on Stratford Upon Avondale's two renowned stages. The five-month long Shakespeare festival is the town's *raison d'être.*

In my short time in the village I had already attended three plays—two Shakespeare and one production of *Arsenic and Old Lace.*

Yes, that was indeed plenty of murder and scandal, and the festival had just begun.

"Morning, Maggie," called out Mrs. Vachon from the souvenir shop three doors down the street, where she was meticulously sweeping the sidewalk. After a few days of clouds and rain, the morning sun felt warm and welcome, and I noticed Mrs. Vachon wasn't the only merchant outside tidying up.

"Good morning." I waved at the energetic, gray-haired woman who'd been running her shop for over forty years.

Maggie O'Flynn—I was the newbie in town. Most of the business owners in the town dedicated to all things Shakespeare and England,— despite being five thousand miles from English soil—had been here for years. Yet they all welcomed me with open arms when I purchased the Merry Wives Tea Room and settled into their town.

Back inside my lace-bedecked, cozily cluttered tea room, I went to the large mirror hanging over the fireplace and with a hair elastic did my best to pull back and tame my light red, insanely wavy hair. It had worked up a nice halo of frizz while I'd baked the day's tea treats. The frizz halo added nearly two inches to my five foot seven inch height. A late night the night before left my green eyes a little red and the wisp of mascara wasn't going to fool anyone.

Finally, I tied on the white apron before whispering my daily 'thank you' to my late Great Aunt Flora. Despite the sad disappointment she believed I had become when, five years earlier at the age of thirty, I had my Great Life Epiphany, she still bequeathed me the generous inheritance which allowed me to buy the tea room. Thanks sent on their way, I busily prepared for my first customers of the day. Without fail, the tourists who stayed at the various B and B's and hotels always needed that mid-morning cup of tea to get them on their way for a day of sightseeing, shopping, and Shakespeare.

I was serving a couple their tea and scones with English clotted cream and homemade strawberry jam when Nate Larimer, owner of the shop next door—Friar's Book Shoppe—came in wearing a broad smile. "Enjoy your cuppa," I told the couple as I turned to greet Nate.

"It's after ten. Shouldn't you be opening your store?" I inquired, a teasing smile on my lips.

"Frank's got it. Just thought I'd catch you early and ask if you wanted to meet for a beer over at the Garter, after you've closed this afternoon." Brows raised in question, the big smile waned a bit as he awaited my reply. A pleasant flirtation had begun the very day I took over the tea room, but the relationship had remained at the flirtation stage for the four months I'd been a resident. Probably for the best, since I was busy starting up my business. However, every time I looked at that six foot two inch, thirty-eight year old man, who could have been a cowboy model if you just put some chaps and a cowboy hat on him, I wished we could perhaps progress a little beyond flirtation. A fantasy or two of running my fingers through the thick, brown hair on his handsome head might have hit me on occasion.

Shaking off the tempting image, I said, "Sure. Why not. Yeah. Sounds good." I was always so articulate around Nate. "Um, I'll come by the shop after I close up."

Just as he was opening his mouth to answer, a woman stepped through the doorway and in a full, strident voice, demanded, "I need a table. Now." She didn't direct her words to my employee, Laura, or me; she simply announced it to the room.

Older than me, probably in her early forties, dressed in a rose colored business suit, make-up hiding any peek of the real face underneath, and features pulled tight from obvious plastic surgery, every eye in the room was on her. It was as if the six customers, along with Laura, Nate, and myself were all holding our breaths as we waited for whatever was going to come next.

I stepped over to her and softly said, "Of course. Please follow me." I led her to a table along the wall, away from the other diners. Queen Elizabeth in her official Jubilee portrait looked down on the woman from her spot on the wall above the table.

"Who are you?" she snapped. "I've never seen you here before." Her eyes traveled from my unruly hair already escaping its elastic, to my sensible—on my feet all day—black shoes.

"I'm Maggie O'Flynn, the new—"

"Whatever. I don't really care who the hell you are. I just need tea, a slice of quiche, and some fruit." I stood there, staring at her, and she barked, "Now. I haven't got all day, you know."

Laura stepped up to the table. "I've got this, Maggie. Ms. Andrews here is a yearly visitor to the town, and I can handle…things." She sounded like someone who had found dog poo on their shoe and was resigned to the necessary clean up. Laura McGrady had worked at the tea room for years before I bought it, and was without a doubt the reason I'd managed to get it running without any hitches right from the start. She was nothing less than a saint. In her early sixties but not looking a day over fifty, she wore her salt and pepper hair in a stylish bob and had a slender, fit physique.

"So, is *someone* going to bother serving me?"

"You'll have your food in just a few minutes," Laura answered through gritted teeth.

I stepped away from the table, but kept my eyes riveted on the nasty woman. I hadn't taken three steps before I saw her eyes light on Nate, who still stood off to the other side of the room.

"Larimer," she shouted across the small room. "Come over here."

He folded his arms over his chest and slowly sauntered over to her. His plaid shirt and nicely fitting jeans added to my cowboy fantasy as I watched him carefully approach the woman.

"I got a book as a gift last night, like I need another book of Shakespeare, and want to return it. Obviously it had to come from your shop, so I'll be dropping it off later. I expect a full refund. Not like I bothered even opening it up."

"Fine," he said in a monotone.

As I headed into the kitchen I grabbed Nate's arm and dragged him along with me. Once we were behind the closed door I asked, "So who the heck is *that?* She obviously knows you, so fill me in."

He took a deep breath and let it out slowly, before answering. "That would be none other than Cressida Andrews, theater critic." He flicked a bit of invisible lint off his shirtsleeve. "She writes for the Tribune, you know, the big regional paper here. Every year at this time she blows into town like a tornado leaving destruction in its wake."

"Well, she's just delightful," I said, my words oozing sarcasm. "So, does she know everyone around here?"

"Pretty much. I think she's been coming here close to ten years."

It occurred to me I had never asked Nate how long he'd lived here, and posed the question now.

"Let's see, about four years. Yeah, that would be about right."

"Was that when you bought the bookshop?"

"No, I'd been here for almost a year before I bought the shop. Worked in the Garter for a bit, and did my carpentry work, of course."

I had seen some of his carpentry work and it was beautiful. When he first divulged his talent to me he explained that he did the type of carpentry you could see, not hidden behind drywall—so cabinetry, gorgeous built-in bookcases, even the occasional piece of furniture.

"I need to get back out there. But if you want to avoid Hurricane Cressida you can sneak out the back."

"Think I'll take you up on that," he said with a smile. "See you about five?"

"If it's quiet I'll leave it to Casey and Laura to close up, so it could be as early as four-thirty. That okay?" Casey Butler was my part-time help who came in at noon each day.

He gave me a wink. "Couldn't be better." And he was out the kitchen's back door.

After the morning with Hurricane Cressida, the afternoon seemed downright dull. It was the usual parade of tourists looking for the quintessential British experience: a proper tea. Most didn't know a Darjeeling from an Earl Grey, but all needed it and needed it now. The steaming pots of tea, scones with clotted cream, and tiered tea trays overflowing with tea sandwiches and sweet treats came out of the kitchen in a constant procession.

The dull peace and tranquility came to a sudden halt with the arrival of my friend and neighbor. All of five foot two inches tall, with long, thick hair the color of espresso, Gina Mattucci always owned whatever room she stepped into. Everything about her was larger than life, from her voice to her gesturing, which often involved her entire arms. I'd been whacked in the head more than once while Gina was in the thralls of telling a story about something that amused her.

She came in, grabbed me by the arm and pulled me back to the kitchen. There she stood with her hands on her hips, working the six-inch stilettos she wore. Her skirt was so short it should have been illegal, and the false eyelashes told me she was dressed for a date. Casey, who was putting the finishing touches on a service of tea sandwiches and cakes, stopped what she was doing to eye Gina.

"Look at me," Gina said as she made a slow spin. "What do you see missing?" Her voice was deep and raspy in a sexy way. I secretly coveted it.

"The rest of your skirt?" Casey offered teasingly, looking just like the pixie her short haircut was named for. Tiny, trim, and blond, she could have been a wood sprite.

"No, this skirt is smokin'." She ran her hands down the skirt, smoothing it into place, while wiggling her hips.

She struck a few poses. "Hint. Look at my ears. If that's not enough of a clue, look at my earlobes." She pushed her hair back to expose the earlobes.

"No earrings," I said.

"Well done, Sherlock. I can't find my favorite hoops. This outfit is incomplete without the hoops. The big ones."

Casey and I stared at her.

"Can I borrow yours, Maggie? You know the ones I mean, the giant silver ones?"

"Sure. You have the key to my apartment, just go ahead and help yourself. I think they're sitting on my dresser."

"Thanks. And, uh, one more thing, if you've got a second." Gina bit on her pouty lower lip, as if nervous. A highly confident thirty-something, I had rarely seen a nervous Gina.

"Yeah, what's up?"

She glanced over at Casey, and back to me, brows lifted.

"Uh, Casey, the tray looks perfect. Why don't you go ahead and take it out to table seven, please?" I said.

"Sure thing. I can take a hint." She giggled as she lifted the tiered tea stand filled with the delicate tea sandwiches and teacakes all artfully arranged and slowly and carefully made her way to the door.

When the door closed behind Casey, Gina leaned in and said, "I could really use a favor. Giant favor. I got laid off yesterday. The company is downsizing." Gina worked as an administrative assistant at a P.R. firm in town. "I already have some feelers out for a new job and I'm sure something will come through soon. But in the meantime I could use a little income." She pushed her hair back from her face. "You think you could use a little help here for a week or two?" She smiled manically, showing gritted teeth.

I debated making her sweat a bit. The truth was I had been considering hiring another person. When I bought the business I was afraid of spending too much on wages, and had hired the bare minimum number of employees I could get by with. It was becoming apparent I had underestimated, and would need another full time employee. However, I was hoping for someone for the long term, not a temporary situation.

"Two weeks, huh?" I asked.

Gina rocked her head back and forth, weighing the situation. "Yeah, I think so."

"What if I said I needed a longer commitment?"

"I love you, Maggie, you know that. But I would never be able to live on what I'd make here. Not in the long run."

Thinking two weeks with Gina would give me time to find the right person for the job without rushing the process, I made my decision.

"Yes. You can come work here for two weeks." Gina's face lit up. "But. I want the full two weeks. And I would need you to start before the shop opens, to help with the prep work. So the hours would be seven to four. That work for you?"

She grabbed me by the shoulders, pulled me in and gave me kisses on both cheeks. "Thank you, thank you, thank you," she said as she tried to wipe bright red lipstick off my face.

"When can you start?"

"Tomorrow too soon?"

"Nope. Meet me here at seven. Oh, and that," I waved a hand at her skimpy skirt and stilettos, "isn't going to work here. You'll need a simple, *modest*, knee-length black skirt, or slacks, and a plain white blouse," I said, indicating with a sweep of my hand, the clothes I wore. "I'll supply the white apron. And comfortable shoes unless you want to be in excruciating pain all day."

She saluted me. "Yes, ma'am." Then with a full-throated laugh, she added, "You know what? This is going to be fun!"

I smiled at her, hoping she was right, and fearing I'd just made a big mistake.

By four-fifty Nate and I were comfortably settled at a table in a quiet corner of The Garter Inn, beers sitting in front of us on the small, round wooden pub table. The Garter was one of two pubs in this town of all things English, so the interior was authentic, right down to the timbered low ceilings and cheerful proprietor. It was still early, but soon the rooms would be noisy and filled with the laughter of both tourists and locals. The other pub, The Robin Goodfellow Public House, known by the locals as 'The Robin', was far more quiet, though still so English you would never know you weren't in Jolly Ol' England.

I took a long swallow of my beer, and peered up at Nate. Our eyes met, and I found myself quickly going to fantasyland. Glancing away in the hope of banishing the scene playing in my mind I asked, "So did Cressida come by to get her refund? And by the way, what kind of name is Cressida? I'll bet it's as real as the dewy fresh look of her face."

"Yeah, but let's not bring that witch into our evening. I've been looking forward to this all day." He reached out his hand and let it briefly rest on mine where it lay on the table.

Hazarding a look into those golden green eyes, I said, "Me too."

We shared our workdays, and discussed the current Shakespeare comedy playing in the Globe, as the Shakespearean theater was known. Much smaller than the one built recently in London, the people of Stratford Upon Avondale were very proud nonetheless, because theirs was built back in the late fifties, thus beating London by almost fifty years.

"I need something new to read, Mr. Bookshop Owner.

Any recommendations?" Sipping my beer, I kept my eyes on his while I awaited his answer.

"You know, it's always so easy to recommend books to you, Maggie. Your tastes are so eclectic." I took this comment as a compliment, as my eclectic tastes had been carefully nurtured over the past five years—ever since the 'Epiphany.' Prior to then, no one would have accused me of being an omnivorous reader.

"I think you'd like what I'm reading right now, *The Indian Year*, about a British family who spends a year in India," and he went on to enthusiastically sell me on the book.

By the time we finished our pints, the room was crowded and the bar area was standing room only. Several tables over I saw a round, florid man dressed in a suit which had seen better days, shaking a finger in the face of none other than Ms. Cressida Andrews. She rolled her eyes at him, leaned in to say something, shoved her chair back, and stood. Turning her back on the man she stomped over to the bar area, where she pushed her way through the crowd until she made it to the bar itself. The man she'd left tipped his head back to finish the last several swallows of his cocktail. By the looks of him, it hadn't been his first.

"Care for another?" Nate asked.

"Oh, why not? And maybe, a basket of chips?" In keeping with the authentic English pub theme, customers had to order their drinks at the bar, and Nate made his way over to it.

As a devout people watcher, I sat back and enjoyed the show the Garter's customers put on. My eyes wandered to the door just as two men walked in. I recognized them from the theater—one was a producer who had visited the tea room a few times, and the other an actor who was in one of the two Shakespeare plays currently running at the Globe. The actor, British, reminded me of the British actor who starred in one of my favorite gritty English detective shows. He was tall, leggy, had dark umber skin, wore his black hair close cropped, and had a VanDyke style beard. Simply put, he was gorgeous. I had just seen him in the play, and his voice was almost as mesmerizing as his looks. I allowed my eyes to linger on him for a few seconds before I was caught. Our eyes met, and rather than quickly looking away, we both let the moment last longer than one normally does. The corner of his mouth went up in a half smile, and I made myself tear my eyes away.

Fortunately, Nate returned just seconds later.

He was wiping his face on a towel. The scent of alcohol wafted off of him.

"What happened to you?" I nearly shouted.

"Cressida happened to me. Didn't you see the ruckus at the bar?"

Uh, no. My eyes were on the hot actor.

"No," I answered, voice all innocence. "I guess I wasn't looking that way. You know me and my people watching." I shrugged to punctuate my point. "So tell me what happened."

"The short version is she said something snarky to me, I may have called her a nasty old witch, or something similar that rhymes with witch, and she threw her drink in my face." He made it sound like it was the kind of thing that happened every day—nothing to make much of a deal about.

But Cressida wasn't finished yet, for just then she and the producer started in on a shouting match. The louder they got the quieter the room became. I caught a few snippets of it, things such as Cressida yelling, "you're just a no-talent has-been who has no business…" and the producer saying "If I ever stage *The Taming of the Shrew* I'll make sure you get the title role…" Cressida's words sounded slurred, and she appeared to be swaying on her feet.

Nate leaned toward me and said, "She's certainly on a roll tonight. Making friends all over the place today, she is."

We watched as the pub's owner and manager, Steve Talbott, came around from behind the bar, and resting one hand on her arm, spoke to her in a voice too quiet for us to hear. He started guiding her to the door as he continued talking. Once she was out of the pub, the noise level in the room returned to normal, as if the curtain had just come down at the end of a play.

With perfect timing, our beers and chips were delivered to our table. I knew our waitress, Courtney, and asked her if this kind of thing happens very often at the Garter.

She laughed. "No, unless it's Cressida season. That woman is just a piece of work. I mean, I've known her most of my life, my mom is an old friend of hers, from college I guess, but that doesn't mean I don't think she's a nasty old cow."

"If what I've seen of her today is any indication, I'd have to agree with you," I said.

"You want to just go ahead and order some dinner? Stay a while?" Nate asked.

I heartily agreed with the plan, and ordered a chicken pasty with salad while Nate asked for the fish and chips. Good, basic pub food. Just like in Merry Ol' England.

The sun was preparing to set, infusing the world with a golden hue, as Nate and I left the pub and started to walk across the town square. Actually shaped more like the top of a grand piano, 'square' probably wasn't the term the founders should have chosen. But it was undeniably attractive, with trees, beds of flowers, and a splashing ornamental fountain near the narrow end. Benches were placed here and there, and a bronze statue of the bard himself sat smack dab in the middle of it all. Early spring flowers were planted in a circle at the base of the statue. Though many of the current crop of visitors were in the theaters at this hour, there were still quite a few people walking through the square enjoying the relative quiet of the evening.

"Do you need to check anything at the tea room before you go home?" Nate asked.

"No, I'm just going to head home."

"I'll walk you."

No argument from me there.

When we got to Shakespeare's bronze statue, we turned right to head to the wider end of the square. Walking closely side by side his hand was just inches from mine and I wished and prayed he would take it in his. Chiding myself for my Nineteenth Century ways, I reached out and took his hand. I felt him jump and peeked up at him. A warm smile and a gentle squeeze of my hand were my answer. I looked down at the bricks and smiled to myself. *Well done, Maggie.*

The square is circled by a road, Hamlet Loop Drive, which we crossed in order to walk down Montague Avenue. Along the way we passed The Robin Goodfellow, which, unlike the Garter, was as quiet as a church.

We turned a corner onto Othello Place and into the quiet residential area where I lived. Though the center of town drips with faux-English charm, anything built away from it still oozes the charm of the early Twentieth Century when the first iteration of the town was founded on the banks of the Avondale River. In those days the town was known as Grantville.

We arrived at the small mansion built at the turn of the last century which now housed five modest apartments— one of which I called home. I plotted my next moves.

"Thank you for seeing me home," I said, turning to face Nate but not letting go of his warm hand.

"Of course."

An awkward silence. It was now or never. Gazing up into those sexy eyes, I grabbed a fistful of his shirt and pulled him close. I let go of his hand and put my hand on the back of his head, leading it down to mine. His breath was warm on my face as I inched my mouth closer to his. When our lips finally made contact it was like I'd been shocked with static electricity. We allowed the kiss to linger, as if neither of us wanted to be the one to end it. But as the instigator I finally did end it, though I kept my eyes closed for several seconds as I listened to him breathe deeply.

Regretfully opening my eyes, I whispered, "I've wanted to do that for a long time."

His eyes opened to half mast, and finding mine he said, "Me too. I just wasn't sure how you felt. I mean, with your background and all, I wasn't sure."

My whole body stiffened, and I let go of his shirt. "What do you mean, 'my background'?" When I saw the nervous look on his face I added, "What do you know about my background? And how do you know it? I mean, if you know something? Or if there's something to know?" My mouth and my brain weren't communicating very well as my brain was busy sending out loud alarms to the rest of my body, making my heart race and my ears ring.

"Don't get mad at her, I'm sure she didn't think she was sharing something she shouldn't," he started as I raised my brows like a teacher waiting for a miscreant student to confess. "It was Laura. We were just chatting one day in my shop and it came up. That's all."

"So…what exactly did she tell you?" I clenched my teeth.

His eyes were wandering, looking anywhere but into mine. "Well, she, uh, told me how you used to be…a nun." He spit out the last words as if to make sure I couldn't hear them. Huh! Oh, I heard them, Nate.

"Novice nun! Nun-in-training! I never took my final vows! And that all ended five years ago." I was breathing hard, like I'd just run a race.

My past life wasn't a secret, but it was also something I didn't usually share with people, mostly because it was the kind of thing that didn't just come up casually in a conversation. And it certainly didn't come up with men I was interested in. And there had been men since I'd left the convent. After all, I had some catching up to do after nearly five years with the sisters.

Nate looked startled at my outburst, as he rested one of his large, warm hands on my upper arm. "Glad that's out in the open. And message received loud and clear. But, in my defense," he paused making sure my eyes were meeting his, "when a man hears something like that, it makes him slow himself down, way, way down. I didn't want to be the man who stole your virtue or something."

I couldn't help myself, and let out a loud laugh. Poor Nate. What a sweet guy, and so endearingly innocent and naive.

"That funny, huh?" He sounded wounded.

I scrunched up my face and tilted my head to one side. "Let's just say, I haven't been living the life of a nun for the past five years."

A bit of pink bloomed on his face.

"It's okay," I reassured him. "I just want it to be clear that I'm a normal, healthy, warm-blooded thirty-five year old woman."

He smirked. "Got it." The bloom on his cheeks intensified into a rich shade of red.

Smiling at him, I said, "Good. I'm really glad to hear that. Because now maybe, you won't feel like you have to act like an altar boy around me anymore."

His response was a quick kiss, followed by what could only be described as a lascivious smile.

"So, why did you leave? What made you decide against a life as Sister Maggie?" I could hear the suppressed laughter in his voice.

"I'm not good at taking orders. In fact I always suspected the nuns spent a lot of time behind my back singing How Do You Solve A Problem Like Maggie?"

At that we both laughed. Air thoroughly cleared now, I kissed his cheek and let myself into the building's large front door.

With a pleasant warmth working its way through my body, I let myself into my apartment, and turned on the lamp that sat on the table next to the door. My flat consisted of four small rooms: a compact living room decorated in Early Goodwill, a teeny, tiny kitchen, a cozy bedroom with a window looking out onto the garden of the house next door, and a utilitarian bathroom. After stopping in the kitchen to start the electric kettle, I made my way to the cluttered desk in the living room, sat down, and opened my laptop. With fresh inspiration on my mind, my fingers danced across the keyboard, pausing only long enough to make a cup of tea when the kettle whistled.

~ two ~

S TILL IN A GIDDY MOOD the next morning, I chose to leave my apartment early and stroll along the river walk before going into the shop to start the first batches of baking. After the pleasant outcome of my evening with Nate, I thought some time communing with nature was just the way to continue my cheery mood. A bucolic park with a paved path follows the Avondale River for a nice distance along the river's bend as well as some of the straightaway. Stratford Upon Avondale sits comfortably tucked into the crook of the river, overlooking the park.

With dawn close the sky began to lighten, revealing another cloudless day on its way. A woodsy scent perfumed the still air. Birds, ready to greet the dawn, tried to find mates by singing their best 'come hither' songs.

The entrance to the park closest to my home was at the southern end, in the straightaway section. I strolled up to the wrought iron archway marking the entrance, but found my way blocked by Casey. Energy visibly shot off of her, and her face was flushed.

"Morning," I greeted her, as if encountering a skittish kitten.

I barely got the word out when the excited Casey nearly shouted, "A body! There was a body found by the river!"

"What? When?" This idyllic village which I'd made home shouldn't have bodies found by the river.

"Just a couple of hours ago, I think. Well, that's when Rob got the call." Her husband, Rob, was one of the small handful of police officers that protected the town.

"Do you know whose body?"

"That's the really weird part. It was that critic, Cressida Andrews."

The woman I had so recently been thinking evil thoughts about. Dead. Guilt swept over me, for my nasty thoughts.

"Have you heard anything about how it happened?"

"Rob just told me it looks like she must have tripped, fallen along the riverbank, with her head landing in the water, face down. So she probably drowned. He says she reeks of alcohol, so most likely a drunken trip and then passed out."

No one, not even someone as unpleasant as Cressida, deserves to have their days end in such a horrible way.

"They're just waiting for the morgue van to get here, so the park is closed for now," she explained.

"Yeah, of course. Poor soul. Very nasty piece of work, but still, poor woman." I wrapped my arms around myself, feeling a sudden chill.

The sun was just starting to peek up over the horizon. Before I left the apartment I had briefly thought twice about taking my walk along the river in the near dark. Whoever found the body must have been out in the full dark.

"Who found her? Do you know?"

"A visitor to town. Older man. Staying at the Twelfth Night. Rob said he was shaking he was so upset by it all."

"Isn't it a little weird to walk in the dark, in an unfamiliar town?"

"I know, you'd think so, right? But there's always people out along the river early in the morning. Runners mostly." Landscape lamps set low to the ground were spaced every fifty feet or so, but they only lit portions of the pavement, not the entire area. They certainly didn't cast much light.

After further chatting about the horrible event—though exciting in its own ghoulish way—I said my good-byes to Casey and backtracked before walking to my shop. At least I could get an early start on the baking and meet Gina for her orientation. I always had an early delivery to make to the Anne Hathaway's Cottage Bed and Breakfast. Ruth Williams, the proprietress, liked to serve my fruited scones at breakfast, and for a change I wouldn't be rushing to get to her on time.

Back in the tea room after my morning delivery, my mind kept wandering back to the unfortunate end of Cressida Andrews. Did she have family? Was anyone attempting to contact them? Would someone with her temperament and personality be missed? Then the larger, more existential questions hit me, such as: What exactly was it that I wanted out of this life? Would anyone mourn me should I suddenly die? Was it getting too late for this thirty-five year old woman to have a family of my own? A gloom started to take over my usually optimistic attitude, and I had to fight it off like the devil. When Gina stepped through the door after running an errand for me I very nearly hugged her, I was so happy to see another soul.

As the morning got underway a theme emerged, as everyone seemed to have heard about the death by the river, and had a great need to share the news and ponder aloud its ramifications. I obviously wasn't the only person in the village to have death on the mind.

The tea room was full with the early lunch crowd when Casey hurried through the front door, breathing heavily as if she'd run miles to get there. It would have been understandable had she been late, but it was still a half an hour before her shift started. And she was coming in through the front door rather than the back. I moved quickly to the door to intercept her.

"What in the world? You're early, my friend. No need to run."

"No, no, it's not that," she said in a stage-style whisper. "Maybe we should go into the kitchen."

I didn't question her, and let her lead the way to the back. Once there, she spoke so fast it was hard to follow along.

"Murder. It was a murder! The medical examiner just

called Rob and told him. Says it looks like someone hit her over the head with something, then she fell, ending up with her face in the water." She paused to take a much needed breath. "She still would have been alive when she fell because she for sure did drown. Water in her lungs." She panted from the effort to get all those words out at high speed.

"Oh my God. That's awful." I shook my head as I studied the tile floor.

"So, you know what that means?" Casey didn't wait for me to answer, but rushed ahead, "It means that someone here is a murderer."

"Yes," I stretched the word out. "Or, it means that someone murdered her and is now miles and miles from here." My secret hope. "I'm going to go out on a limb here and guess that this is the first murder in this adorable little village in a long, long time, right? Maybe the first since Rob started working here?"

She nodded. Sparks of excitement flew off of her. If Sister Juliana were there she would have seen a brilliant red aura surrounding Casey, no doubt. Sister Juliana, from my convent days, claimed the ability to see auras. Whether I believed her or not I never decided.

"You want to take the afternoon off?" I asked, worried she wouldn't be able to focus on her work.

"Yes. I mean no. Or maybe I should." Her brow furrowed with the decision-making. "No. I really shouldn't. I should be here. That way I'll be right here in town in case there's more information to get, like news of an arrest." The Butlers lived a mile outside of the Shakespeare part of the town. Obviously much too far from the murder scene for Casey's liking.

"Okay, but why don't you sit down here in the kitchen and let me get you a cup of tea. You just relax with it until you feel like you're ready to work." I started making the tea while I spoke, taking away the need for her to make yet another decision.

This latest news spread quickly, and as the afternoon went on, Merry Wives Tea Room appeared to be the place to exchange information on the murder. Of course, I'm sure if I'd been at either of the pubs, I would have seen the same phenomenon occurring. The sad truth is that small town homicides are good for business if your business serves food and drink.

We didn't have to wait long for news of a suspect.

Needing a break from the constant murder chatter in the tea room, I slipped out for a few minutes and went next door to Nate's shop and what I hoped would be a quiet, murder-talk-free atmosphere. The shop was quiet, reinforcing my theory about folks gathering at the village watering holes to share murder gossip.

Frank stood at the register, and not seeing Nate I went up to him to ask about his whereabouts.

He sucked in his lips before finally revealing Nate's location. "In back. The office." He nodded rhythmically. I stood and watched him, knowing more had to be coming. "Police just left," he whispered. "They've been questioning him. You know, about this murder thing."

My eyes decided to cease focusing, and my ears felt as if they were stuffed with cotton.

I squinted at Frank, trying to bring his round face and bald pate into focus. "What?" I barely got the one syllable out—my lungs had no air in them.

"I haven't had a chance to talk to him yet. They literally just left, right before you came in. He's still here, so they didn't arrest him."

Forcing enough air into my lungs to utter one sentence, I asked, "You think it would be okay if I went back and saw him?"

"Yeah, sure. Probably a good idea."

Not having a clue what I would say to him, I started slowly making my way past the shelves of books and to the back office.

Through the window in the door I saw Nate leaning his elbows on his desk, head held in his hands. I knocked twice, as gently as I could. He turned his head toward me and lifted one hand to gesture me in.

I closed the door quietly behind me as if trying not to startle the man in the room, and said, "Nate?"

"Hey."

"What's going on? Frank said something about a visit from the police." My voice is usually fairly high in the decibel scale, something that never went over well in the convent, but now I used the softest, most gentle voice I could muster.

"Yep."

"You want to talk about it?"

A chair sat against the wall and I pulled it over to the desk and sat down close to Nate. His eyes didn't make contact with mine. He sighed a couple of times while I waited for him to say something.

"Well…" Another sigh. "Looks like I'm prime suspect number one." He rubbed his face with both hands and ran his fingers through his hair.

"Why? Why would they think you had anything to do with it?"

"A few people at the Garter mentioned to Rob Butler that Cressida and I had that little argument that ended with her throwing her drink in my face."

"But that isn't enough to suspect you of *murder*! And there were other people last night who had heated arguments with her, too. So why you?"

"Yeah, Rob knows about those other arguments too. But, well…"

I leaned forward, waiting for him to finish the thought, as my heart beat erratically in my chest.

"But well what?"

"They found Cressida's cell phone, and I guess there were a bunch of calls to my phone in it."

"She called you?" I instantly regretted the surprise in my voice.

He stared at his hands.

"I guess."

"Why? And didn't you see that she called you?" This time I sounded accusatory, and again I instantly regretted it.

His eyes met mine, and they weren't happy looking.

27

"Of course I saw that she called me, Maggie." Oops, I might have gone too far. "I ignored the calls."

I wanted so badly to ask the obvious, but with those narrowed eyes drilling into me I was afraid asking would be a mistake. Unfortunately, impulse control had never been my strong suit, another reason why the nuns and I weren't so copacetic. "But, *why* would she be calling *you*?"

"You know, I'm starting to see that what they say about redheads is the truth." Okay, I definitely went too far. *Impulse control, Maggie!*

I sat up, leaning as far from him as I could in the tight quarters.

He closed his eyes and slowly let out a breath. When he opened his eyes they were sad puppy dog eyes. "I'm sorry. I don't really mean that. It's just been a lousy morning."

"I know. I can only imagine how awful it must have been to have the police in here. But they left and didn't take you with them, so they must have believed you when you said you had nothing to do with the murder."

"You believe that I didn't do it?"

"Of course! Oh my God, of course I know you wouldn't have killed her." I placed my hand on his where it rested on his knee.

"Well, Rob isn't completely convinced that I didn't do her in. When he left he made sure I knew I'd be seeing him again soon."

"That's horrible! No, he has to know you wouldn't. You couldn't." I was reaching my usual decibel level.

"It's okay, Maggie. I'm sure he's just doing his job."

I shook my head. "No way. I think we need to prove you didn't do it, and then he can move on and find the real killer."

"He'll come to that conclusion. He has to, since I didn't kill her."

I got quiet, busy thinking.

"You want to meet up later?" I asked. "Maybe I could make you dinner?"

He smiled for the first time since I got there. "That would be very, very nice. I have to be here till eight, so would eight, eight-thirty be okay?"

My brain quickly worked on a plan for the rest of my day, and I decided his time frame would work well for what I had to accomplish before I saw him at eight.

"Perfect. I'll see you then." I should have stood up and left the office. But I found myself staring at the curvy lips in front of me, and memories of last night rushed to my mind. Would it be wrong to just lean forward and give them a friendly little kiss? I must have thought too long about it, because the decision was made for me when he leaned over to me and gave me a soft, warm kiss. Brief. Not the Great Passion. But also decidedly not a kiss you would give your grandmother.

I stood, replaced the chair, and opened the door. With a smile I said, "See you tonight," and left the room with the smile still on my lips. It stayed right there until I got to the self-help section, and the realization hit me.

Nate never did answer my question about why Cressida would have repeatedly called him.

***

As I entered my warm kitchen at the tea room, the aroma of good, strong English tea assailed me. Prescribing myself a cup for what ailed me I poured the cup and added a few drops of milk. I even sat down for a minute or two to savor it, allowing the scented steam to caress my face. Only when I felt the nervous edge that had gripped me in Nate's office, begin to dissipate, did I leave the comfort of the kitchen and head out into the still busy tea room.

Casey saw me first and hurried through serving tea to a dapper elderly couple. Finished at their table, she made her way over to me.

"One of the ladies over there," she said, pointing at a table by the front window, "says that 'the nice young man who runs the bookshop' has been arrested." Her eyes became massive saucers in her delicate face.

"I need to go call Rob," she added.

I gently laid a hand on her shoulder, attempting to calm her. "No, you don't need to. I was just over there, and though he was questioned, no one arrested Nate."

"Is he a suspect?" Gina appeared suddenly at my elbow.

We stood in the middle of the room, with several tables within hearing distance. Taking Casey's hand and putting a hand on Gina's shoulder, I led them to the back of the room, near the kitchen door.

"I think so. But he didn't do it."

"No," Casey chuckled nervously. "Nate wouldn't kill anyone. Not even someone as horrid as that Cressida."

"I know. But I just want to make doubly sure that your husband and his colleagues know that too."

"What do you mean?" Gina said, attempting, yet failing, to lower her voice.

"I don't think it would hurt any to find some way to prove he didn't do it," I explained.

This got Gina's attention. She grabbed my shoulders. "Yes! That's what we should do! Oh, we could do our own investigating, and find the real murderer, and then Nate would be, what's the word? Um, exonerated!" It seemed she'd given up on trying to keep her voice down.

How we got from *me* to *we* I didn't know, and my first inclination was to set her straight and tell her I would handle things. But then I realized that having someone helping me who had lived here for more than five minutes would probably be helpful. Before continuing this chat my eyes scanned the full room. Laura stood at a table for two, taking an order. For the moment she had things under control, but the three of us needed to wrap this up.

"I want to help too!" Casey whined.

"How would Rob feel about you doing that?" I asked.

She rolled her eyes. "What Rob doesn't know won't hurt him."

It was that kind of thinking that could get a woman threatened with expulsion from a convent. And very likely could do harm to a marriage.

"No, I don't want you doing something that would upset Rob. I'm sure he doesn't want you messing with people who could be dangerous." Though it would be helpful to have the conduit of information that we could get from Rob through Casey.

She stared at me for several long seconds. "Whatever!"

I shook my head and looked to the ceiling. "Okay, but look. Let me do some legwork, then we'll review anything I find out. Then, and only then, will we decide if we should continue."

I could see Casey thinking it over. Gina had clearly made up her mind that we would be conducting our own investigation.

"Yeah, yeah. Okay," Casey agreed.

"Good, now let's get going and help Laura. I have a couple of ideas of things I'd like to find out after we close up this afternoon."

Gina gave me a conspiratorial smile, and headed off to give a customer his check. With my plan beginning to form I looked anxiously over at the ornate Victorian clock on the fireplace mantel. Three hours until closing. I knew it would be the slowest three hours of all time.

⁓ three ⁓

FOUR O'CLOCK FINALLY ROLLED AROUND, the tea room was empty and Casey shoved me out the door, telling me she would close up. "Get going and start gathering information." I feared her enthusiasm would end up getting us in nothing but trouble. But, impatient to get started, I allowed her to have her way and left the Merry Wives to head down to the souvenir shop.

Sarah Vachon, having been in Stratford Upon Avondale for at least forty years, seemed like the best place to start. I hoped she would be able to shed a little light on a thing or two.

I entered the large shop, with its shelves and nooks and bins and display cases brimming full with everything and anything Shakespearean or English. My eye quickly found the spry older woman unpacking a box over in the Christmas ornament section. I had been told during my first visit to the shop a few months ago that the Christmas section was a year-round part of the shop. A large Union Jack pattern decorated both the front and back of Sarah's sweater. Teapot earrings hung from her ears.

"Oh, Maggie. How nice to see you," she greeted me. "Just unpacking these lovely Anne Boleyn ornaments. You know, nothing says Christmas like a beheaded queen!" She laughed at her own joke as I picked one up and found that it thankfully still had its head intact. In fact, it was rather pretty, with its emerald green gown, and delicate headdress encrusted with tiny fake pearls.

"I might just need to add one of these to my ornament collection, Mrs. Vachon."

"Oh, now for the hundredth time, please call me Sarah," she said as she created a new display with the beheaded queen ornaments.

"Sarah. I was wondering if you could help me with something." As I had been walking over I wondered just how I was going to approach this situation without giving myself away entirely. I still had no idea.

"Of course, dear. What is it?"

"I know you've been here for quite a while, and I'm guessing you know something about this poor woman who got murdered, Cressida Andrews."

"Yes, yes, I do indeed. Had my run in with her now and again over the years." Her face took on a pinched, sour lemon look.

"Well, the thing is, as a new resident here, this murder has me kind of nervous." I found myself easily slipping into the lie. "And I'm hoping it isn't a common occurrence to find dead bodies by the river."

Sarah laughed. "You poor dear. No, no, no. This is the first time in my memory, and you know that memory goes way, way back, that we've had a murder here in Stratford."

"Maybe if I knew a little more about her, it would make me feel better about things. You know how they say facts make the nightmares go away." I had never heard such a thing, but my mouth said it on its own.

She stopped what she was doing, and studied me. I might have lied a moment earlier about being nervous, but now under her gaze I did feel a bit anxious.

"Hmmm…" she began. "Never heard that one, myself. But if it will help you, sure I can tell you what I know. She's been coming here once or sometimes twice a year to see the plays and write reviews on them." Closing up the now empty box, she continued, "If I'm not mistaken, rarely was a review straight out complimentary. I mean, there was always some nugget of criticism. And those were just the good ones!" She cackled. "Many were downright mean and nasty."

"That's awful. I'd think in a town that makes its living on its theater that wouldn't be good for the economy."

She shrugged. "Maybe. Back when she was still new at it. But nowadays everyone knows it's just her way."

"Any chance you know where she was staying?"

"Oh, that's easy. She always stayed at The Lady Grey Bed and Breakfast. That would be over there on Titania Lane."

"Yeah, I know the place. I walk by it most days."

"Place is run by Jane Morris. She's been there for a number of years, about as long as Ruth Williams has been at the

35

Hathaway." I'd made the right decision to stop there first, Sarah knew the entire history of the town and its inhabitants.

The bell over the door rang, and Sarah excused herself to greet her customer. I took the opportunity to slip out before she started wondering why I was being so nosy.

After stopping at the tea room's kitchen to pick up some lemon teacakes for Jane Morris, I cut across the town square which took me to Titania Lane. The Lady Grey B and B was a large, late Victorian house that sat overlooking the Avondale River. With its windows at the back of the house looking out over the river, it commanded the best view of any of the overnight accommodations available in the town. It certainly looked like the kind of place Cressida Andrews would require. I hoped my visit would shed some light on what Cressida had been doing in the hours just prior to her murder. Perhaps Ms. Morris would know something about her activities.

A middle-aged woman wearing an apron, no make-up, and sporting two red-rimmed eyes, answered my knock. One hand clutched a facial tissue, while the other pushed graying brown hair away from her face.

"Yes?" Her voice crackled with no hint of hospitality. Which, given the eyes that had so obviously been tear-filled just prior to my intrusion, was not a surprise.

"I'm sorry to bother you. My name is Maggie O'Flynn— I own the Merry Wives. Would you be Ms. Morris?"

"I am." She eyed me suspiciously. I understood the feeling, but I wanted to shout, 'No, I'm not a murderer! And murderers don't come bearing boxes of teacakes!'

"I understand Ms. Andrews was a guest here, and I just wanted to extend my condolences." I had come up with that snappy line as I walked across the square. At the time I'd thought no one would be mourning such an unlikeable woman, but now, seeing those red eyes, I realized that perhaps someone was.

A small sob escaped her throat, and she pressed the tissue to eyes that filled with tears. "How kind of you," she said through the sob.

"I'm sure it must be such a shock."

Those must have been the magic words, for she opened the door wide and waved me in with her free hand.

Offering her the box, I said, "I've brought you some teacakes from my tea room. I thought perhaps you or your guests would enjoy them."

"How sweet of you. Thank you. Would you like some tea, or coffee?" she asked.

The last thing I needed was more tea, but I said, "Yes, please. Some tea would be lovely." Tea meant more time to find out what Jane Morris knew.

She excused herself to go to the kitchen, leaving me in the front parlor. It was appropriately furnished in antiques that fit the style of the house. Doilies, ceramic figurines, and period correct knick-knacks were here and there around the room. But most striking how every inch of the wall space, and the top of every flat surface was covered in photographs. Each one a picture of smiling people: individuals, families, small groups. At the center of each was the same woman at varying ages, young in the black and white pictures, older in the faded color photos, and finally recognizable as Jane Morris in the high resolution pictures of the digital age. She had apparently chronicled her years of guests through photography. And it appeared there had been many, many guests over those years.

While peering at a picture of a family all dressed in Tudor costumes, I heard Jane come into the room.

She set down the tea tray and said, "Aww, I see you're admiring my years of guests."

"It's very impressive." *And just a little too Alfred Hitchcock, or Stephen King for my taste,* I thought to myself.

"They each become like friends, you know." She sounded wistful, and dabbed again at an escaping tear.

"I can imagine."

"Do you take anything in your tea?" she asked returning her attention to the business of tea.

"No, black is fine. So, did Ms. Andrews stay here very often?"

"Every year for the past ten," she answered proudly, but then folded in on herself as she choked back more sobs.

I moved over to her and put my hand on her back. When she didn't move, I started gently patting the spot. After a minute or two, she straightened herself.

"Oh dear, I'm so sorry. She was just such a dear friend."

I hoped my face didn't show the shock I felt at hearing this affection for the woman who seemed universally despised.

"Here, come sit down," I said as I guided her toward a wingback chair.

"I'm sorry. What was your name again?"

"Maggie. Maggie O'Flynn. I recently bought the Merry Wives."

"Maggie. It's nice to meet you. You're so kind." And with that the tears flowed again.

"You know, it helps sometimes if we talk about the ones we've lost." How was that for subtle?

"Yes, yes I think so," she said through hiccups.

"Would you like to tell me about Ms. Andrews?"

"Cressida was a lovely lady, always so generous." I wanted to ask if we were talking about the Cressida Andrews who had just been murdered. The drunken one who had argued with just about everyone in the Garter the night before. "And so smart. You've never met anyone as smart as Cressida. She should have been a much more famous theater critic, you know. Or a great novelist. The way she could use words. And big words too. So many words…" she appeared to drift off to the comfort of a memory.

Returning to me, she continued, "And so beautiful. Always dressed like such an elegant lady." She looked up at me as if with a sudden thought. "Did you ever get to meet Cressida?"

I nodded, while my lips formed a tight-lipped smile. "Yes, I did. She was in my tea room yesterday as a matter of fact." I didn't go into more detail. She wouldn't have believed me if I did. And no need to bring up the problems at the Garter.

"Beautiful, wasn't she? What a true lady she was." She stared into space and I let her have her silence.

"I will miss her, you know," she said, just as I thought I'd lost her for good.

"I'm sure you will." I used my nun-in-training voice, the one that was soft, gentle, and sounded like I had recently had a lobotomy.

It was time to get something more than the argument for Cressida Andrew's canonization to sainthood. "Did you see her last night?" I asked.

Her eyes flickered over to me. "Well, yes."

"Before she went out, or after she returned?" I hoped I wasn't pushing too much. I didn't want to scare her off now.

The question seemed to confuse her. "Oh, before, I suppose."

"Happy memories, right?" *Please stay with me*, I thought.

"Oh yes. We had tea together. Right here in this room. We talked about plays she had seen, and books. You know, all those things she knew so much about. Then she said she had to go out for a while."

"Did you hear her come home?"

"Home. Oh home. Yes, this was a home for her. Yes. Home." She wiped her eyes and nose.

"So you heard her come home?" I lost something in that last bit.

"Oh, no. No." She shook her head. "I go to sleep pretty early. So I didn't hear anything after about nine-thirty."

That was disappointing. My theory that Jane Morris would be able to tell me what Cressida was doing after she left the Garter was shot.

I knew I needed to get going before I said something that

blew my cover. Before leaving, though, I wanted one last thing.

"Could you show me any pictures you have of Cressida?"

I couldn't have asked a better question by the look of joy on Jane's face. She showed me four pictures, each of a scowling Cressida and a beaming Jane, the only things that changed from picture to picture were their ages and clothes.

At the door, on my way out, I said, "Thank you, Jane, for sharing your memories with me. If there's anything I can do please let me know. You can always find me at the Merry Wives." She answered with a hug.

"You were so sweet to come by. It does help to talk about it."

As I walked the half a block to my flat I wondered if I'd just met one of God's most accepting and forgiving people, or one of his most simpleminded and naive.

My money was on simpleminded and naive.

Back at my apartment I checked the time and decided to try calling Gina, who hadn't been home when I knocked on her door. Gina lived in the same converted mansion I did, in the apartment next door to mine. She picked up on the first ring.

"So tell me everything you've found out." Her enthusiasm was palpable through the phone.

"You someplace where you can talk?" I asked.

"Yeah, yeah, just sitting in my car at the drive-through espresso out on the highway. The dang line isn't moving at all." This was punctuated by a moan.

I told her about my visit with Jane Morris and how the Cressida she knew was vastly different from the one everyone else knew. And more to the point, that Jane hadn't seen her later in the evening.

"You know," she said, "Jane could be one of those people who gets so star struck with a well known person that she doesn't really see them for who they actually are. It sounds like she's made a Cressida Andrews who fits her own idea of what a theater critic should be."

It was an insightful observation, and one I hadn't considered. And I hated admitting to myself that I was surprised it came from Gina.

"Maybe. She does seem like the quiet, small town kind of woman whose life is so boring she might just enjoy the excitement someone like Cressida would bring, even if the woman was a witch."

"Exactly. But dang, she didn't see her later in the evening? Can't shed any light on what Cressida was doing down by the river?"

"No. Which is disappointing. If we could find out why she was down there we might find out who she was with. I let myself get too excited that Jane was going to be able to tell us more."

"Yeah, but you just know the police would have talked to her too, and I'll bet you anything they were just as bummed as we are when they didn't get anything from her. No worries. We'll think of other ways to go with it."

"I have some ideas on that score. I was at the Garter when she was causing all kinds of fusses. I mean, Nate wasn't the only one who had words with her. Maybe we should talk to that producer. I'll look him up online, and try to get an appointment to talk to him."

"Good. I'll come in a little early tomorrow and we can talk more then. That is if I ever get out of this freaking line." She suddenly shouted, "Come on people! Let's go!" Returning to me, she said, "Hey, maybe I'll have some great idea over night." She snorted, as if the thought was ludicrous. "You never know! See ya in the morning."

After our goodbyes it was time to turn my attention to getting ready for Nate. I knew he would be distracted by the current situation, but I still had high hopes for this evening, and wanted everything to be perfect.

In the fridge I found the large plastic container of marinara sauce Gina had given me the day before. She could never make just a little of anything her Italian mother had taught her to cook. Living alone, but always making enough food for a family of six, I was often the recipient of her delicious leftovers. After putting it over low heat to allow it to simmer for an hour or so I headed to the bedroom to find just the right outfit.

I went through every hanger in my closet twice before pulling out the little black dress. It was what I had often thought of as my Secret Weapon dress, as I knew just how good it looked on me. It clung to every curve, was cut low in the front, but not too low, was short, but not too short. In other words I looked sexy in it without looking like a hooker. I laid it on the bed not wanting to slip it on until I was finished making dinner.

A look in the mirror convinced me a little product needed to be applied to my frizzy hair. My hair was what my mother always told me was my 'crowning glory.' At that moment the crown was more of a frizzy mess that fell past my shoulders. After I spritzed it with some frizz tamer and ran my fingers through it, I turned my attention to my face. I always allowed my sprinkling of freckles to show—why use cover up on something that only made you look younger? But a little blusher and mascara wouldn't hurt and after admiring the effect I added just a touch of eye shadow to bring out the green in my eyes. There. *Let's see if Mr. Larimer can ignore this version of Maggie*, I thought to myself with a mischievous grin at my reflection in the mirror.

An hour later the aroma of marinara sauce wafted through the flat, and it was time for finishing touches. I put on the Secret Weapon, earrings, and a simple silver necklace, and left my feet bare. After all, something had to look casual and like I wasn't trying too hard.

I went through the living room lighting strategically placed candles, and left only one dim lamp lit. An MP3 player with the help of decent speakers provided mood music. My dining area consisted of a small table at the end of the living room that led into the kitchen. On the table candles burned, and a small bouquet of spring flowers adorned it. I was opening the bottle of wine when I heard the knock on the door.

As I peered through the peek hole, I ran my hands over my dress, smoothing it out. Striking a casual pose I opened the door.

Nate's eyes slowly ran up and down me, clearly taking in a version of Maggie O'Flynn he never saw around the Merry Wives. As if remembering where he was he eventually gave me a warm smile, and with a frog in his throat drawled, "Hi."

"Hi yourself. Come on in."

I had never seen Nate look so awkward and uneasy as he did at that moment, standing in my living room, holding a bottle of wine he seemed to have forgotten he even had. He kept shifting his weight from one foot to the other, eyes scanning the room.

"That for us?" I asked pointing at the bottle. I smiled lazily.

"Oh, yeah. Yeah, it is. I hope it's good. The guy at the wine shop recommended it."

"I'm sure it will be lovely."

His eyes continued to wander the room and when he saw the open wine bottle on the table he said, "Oh no. Wine. Open. Already."

I laughed. "It will hold. What you brought is much better than that. I can drink mine some night this week when I'm sad and lonely," I said as I took the bottle and went into the kitchen to open it. "Make yourself comfortable."

When I returned to the living room a minute later, bottle and two glasses in hand, Nate was sitting on the couch, long legs stretched out in front of him. He wore a pair of black jeans and a blue oxford shirt. I paused to admire the effect.

"It smells delicious in here."

I poured the wine and handed him a glass. "We're having

45

Italian. Spaghetti. The sauce is fantastic, and I can say that because I didn't make it. My crazy Italian friend next door gave me her marinara leftovers."

Arranging myself on the couch next to him, I asked, "So, how are you doing now? Have the police come to their senses and left you alone?"

He took a long sip of the red wine. "I'm okay. I guess. This day wasn't exactly the one I imagined when I woke up. But I'm glad to say I haven't seen Rob or any of his cohorts since that one interview."

"Good. They shouldn't be bothering you."

He adjusted the way he was sitting, then readjusted it before saying, "I never did tell you the rest of the story. You know, why they picked me to question, of all the people at the Garter last night." He looked at me sheepishly, before adding, "And why she was calling me."

No, he hadn't. I put my hand on his knee, and just as quickly removed it. "That's okay. You don't have to tell me anything you don't want to," I lied. Yes, you do need to tell me *everything*, I wanted to shout.

"She had called me three times in just an hour. I kind of guessed why she was probably calling because she did this the last time she was here, too." He paused to take a swallow of wine. "I just ignored the calls, and she didn't even leave a voicemail."

He sniffed. Ran his free hand through his hair. Sucked his lips in. I waited, trying to be patient. After a long sigh he continued, "Cressida has, I mean *had*, a way of trying to collect men in the towns she visited. At the end of her visit last year she decided she wanted to add me to her collection." His eyes glanced my way, as if to assess my reaction. I tried to show no reaction at all, a trick I learned in the convent when I knew I was about to get into trouble for something. "I couldn't imagine anything I would rather not do, but I did let her buy me a beer one night. I don't know why, I guess it was one of those moments of insanity. I spent the next hour fighting her off, and boy, she wasn't a woman who wanted to take no for an answer." He shuddered, making the wine in his glass slosh about.

I wanted to say 'Yuk', but held my tongue. Instead, I said, "That pretty much sounds just like the woman I saw yesterday. She was just a barracuda in all ways, wasn't she?"

He nodded.

"I'm going to go into my teeny-tiny kitchen and start the water boiling for the pasta, and finish the salad, want to come keep me company?" I hoped for some time with Nate in the cramped quarters of the kitchen.

Later, after Nate was a complete gentleman and didn't lay a hand on me in the kitchen, we were half-way through dinner and a comfortable conversation with plenty of laughter when I turned the topic back to Cressida. I told him about the odd visit I had with Jane Morris, and my disappointment that she didn't know anything about Cressida's evening after she left the Garter.

"You aren't trying to investigate this yourself, are you?" The words were tinged with more than a hint of anger.

I examined my pasta as I twirled it onto the fork. Without taking my eyes from my task I answered,

"Well...no...not really. I just happened to be there and so we were chatting about Cressida and the murder. You know, in a neighborly sort of way."

"How did you *happen* to be there?"

"I thought it would be a kind gesture to take some teacakes over for her guests. I'm sure the whole murder thing has to have everyone staying there pretty upset." When lying, always stick as close to the truth as possible. Another lesson learned at the convent. Though certainly not one the sisters had intended on me learning.

I was rewarded with a warm, crooked smile. "Okay, but don't start thinking that you're the next Jessica Fletcher. This is a murder. Which means that someone is a murderer. I don't want you getting hurt." A warmth spread through my body and it wasn't from the wine or the pasta. Nate didn't want me getting hurt. He had to care. I would definitely be trying for a kiss later.

And, fingers crossed, more than a kiss.

By ten-thirty we each had a half of a bottle of wine in us, along with the homey meal, and neither of us was feeling any pain. Talk of the murder ended long ago, and we had settled down on the couch. As we chatted about a new controversial novel by an even more controversial author, I rearranged myself in such a way that I leaned against him.

"You sure you're not cuddling up to a murderer?" he teased as he put his arm around me.

"Would I do this if I thought that?" I leaned over and

placed my lips on his. His hand ran down my side, over my hip and down my thigh before he pulled back and ended the kiss and the caress. It took me a few seconds to register what happened and open my eyes to face whatever was going on in Nate Larimer's mind.

"What? I thought that was…mmmm…nice," I said, catching my breath.

"It was. Very nice. Too nice. I think I should get going."

"No. I mean, you don't need to go. We were both enjoying ourselves, so why stop? And don't give me that line about me being a nun. Not. A. Nun."

"It's been a long day, Maggie. I don't think it would be right. Not now." He let his eyes wander over me, from the red waves, over the curves so evident in the Secret Weapon, and down to my bare toes. "Not that I wouldn't enjoy it. I'm a man, and I have eyes, and they certainly like what they see, but I don't think it would be right. Yet." He gave me a sexy half-smile that made my toes curl.

After extricating himself from me, he stood. "I should get going. Hopefully tomorrow won't include visits from the police. Thank you for a great dinner. And everything else." His eyes met mine and held them. The look warmed me. "Mostly, thanks for taking my mind off the investigation." He slowly made his way to the door.

"Totally my pleasure." I got on tiptoes to kiss his cheek. I let my mouth linger on the stubble and breathed in his scent—musky, manly.

He stepped back and said, "Make sure you lock up. Windows too."

"I'm on the second floor!"

"It wouldn't hurt though, would it?" His brows were raised in a fatherly, do-as-I-say way.

"Okay." No need to fight it.

After I closed the door behind him I didn't hear him step away until I had turned both the locks on the door.

Not until I heard him on the stairs did I lean on the door and let out a long, low, groan.

Thoroughly disappointed, I went over to my desk, opened my laptop and let my frustrations out on my keyboard.

~ four ~

Thursday, May 21st

FTER RETURNING FROM MY DAILY morning delivery trip to Anne Hathaway's Cottage B and B, I placed the key in the lock at the tea room and let out a loud yelp. With a most unexpected hand on my shoulder, Casey shouted in my ear, "They've taken Nate in for more questioning!"

Casey and Gina stood shoulder to shoulder, as if they'd been standing sentry together awaiting my arrival. The telltale flour on Gina's apron told me she'd at least started the morning's baking.

I turned to eye the bearer of this bad news. "What? Now? Why? You mean they actually have him in the police station?" I ran out of air or I might have continued asking rapid-fire questions. Someone had turned on the adrenaline spigot in my body. The room turned unbearably hot.

"Yes! About a half an hour ago. Rob was acting weird last night, then just when he was leaving the house he told me they would be getting Nate first thing this morning."

Gina remained uncharacteristically quiet, arms crossed over her chest, watching my face as Casey filled me in.

I slumped into a chair at one of the front tables. "Did he say why?"

"Not really. Just something about needing to know more about their argument at the Garter. But I overheard him on the phone before he left saying something about needing to know more about their past." Casey raised her brows and bared her teeth in a grimace, like a child who doesn't want to fess up to something.

"They didn't have a *past*." I almost mentioned how Cressida wanted them to have a future, but didn't want that getting back to Rob.

She shrugged. "I don't know anything more. That's just what he said."

"Mr. Hot Devil Bookshop Owner seems to be in a little trouble," Gina announced, her low, gravelly voice making the news sound that much more sinister.

After what Nate said last night I was sure the police would be done with him and moving on to more likely suspects. This news lit a fire under me to keep looking into things myself.

"Casey, big favor to ask. Can you take—"

"Yes!" she said before I finished. "I'll take your spot this morning. You can go be a sleuth!" Watching her twitch with enthusiasm over the situation, I wondered briefly if, as a child, her teachers had found ways to deal with the obvious hyperactivity.

"Thanks. Listen, call Julie first thing and see if she can come in for at least the morning." Julie was my part-part-time employee who filled in as necessary. A retired postal worker, she had too much free time on her hands and always snapped up any hours I could throw her way.

"Do you have any ideas what you're going to do? Who to talk to?" Gina asked.

"I think the best thing to do would be to keep working the Garter angle. I saw two other angry exchanges Cressida had, besides the one with Nate, and that seems like the logical place to start."

"Agreed," Gina said. Casey nodded.

"I know she had words with that producer, I think his name is Kristof something. I don't know who the other man was that I saw her argue with, but I'll bet if I ask Steve he'll know."

"Kristof?" Gina asked, sounding like she'd just taken a swig of milk that had gone bad. "I've seen him around town. Piece of work. Real player." By the tone of her voice I wondered if he'd tried to play with Gina.

Ignoring Gina's comment, Casey said, "Yep, I think you should start with those. If we hear anything we'll call or text you."

"And I think you should be keeping your ears open in here, too," I suggested. "You never know what you might overhear."

"We will," Gina said. "Now get out there and get started."

I looked at the clock. It was only seven-thirty. There was little chance the offices at the theater would be open so early, and I knew Steve didn't get to the pub before nine. There was time to spare.

"Hey, do you know if the police have taken down the crime scene tape down at the river?" I asked Casey.

"I think Rob said they were taking it down this morning."

"Good. It wouldn't hurt to go check out the crime scene while I wait for people to get to work." In truth I had no idea what I could possibly gain by visiting the scene, but I had read enough mysteries to know that it was always done that way.

I gave Casey and Gina directions on the food prep that needed to be done before the tea room opened for the day, and left to begin my sleuthing. After crossing the narrow end of the square I headed to the stairs adjacent to the Globe theater. The stairs led down a small hillside to the river walk. For the third day in a row the sun shone in a nearly cloudless sky, but it was chilly and I drew my jacket tight around me. At the base of the stairs I stood and took in the view. On the other side of the river native old pine trees stood sentinel, while on my side the paved walk was carefully landscaped with deciduous trees that sported new leaves, flower beds, and strategically placed benches. Despite the early hour several people were out enjoying the pleasant morning. Spring had arrived in this area of the world and the birds seemed to know it, as they noisily flirted with one another.

The paved path and landscaping ended several yards from the river itself, leaving a natural riverbank that at this time of year was still muddy from winter and spring rains.

Clumps of native grasses and shrubs grew along this untouched area. Just beyond this section the river rock began. After an unusually dry winter for this area of the country the river was lower than normal for springtime, and a wide swath of rock was exposed.

I turned left and headed to where I'd seen the crime tape. Nothing was left to mark the spot as anything special, and I felt a moment of sadness for the unpleasant death Cressida had met, despite her own unpleasantness. This bit of the natural riverbank was wider than most of it along the path, and I saw rocks of various sizes as well as roots that all could have been obstacles to someone walking there in the dark. But of course, Cressida was helped along in her fall.

Turning my eyes upward I saw the large, elegant homes that sat at the top of the hillside, enjoying their commanding view of the river and the forest on the opposite side. All had large windows to make the most of the view. I found the back of the house that I thought was the Lady Grey. If Cressida had been waiting to meet someone along the river, her B and B would certainly have afforded an excellent place to wait and watch for the person.

Of course. Cressida Andrews was not a woman to go out for a casual late-night stroll along a river, especially not after all the alcohol she had consumed that evening. No, she had to have planned to meet someone. Someone she didn't want anyone to see her with, or why the dark riverside for a meeting place? This realization would need to be further examined more carefully later, for it was eight o'clock now and time to head over to the theater's offices.

Once I got to the top of the stairs I turned left into the theater complex. This pretty, and oh so English area sat just opposite the narrow part of the square, on the other side of the street. The Globe stood majestically on the left, and the modern theater, The Alfred Hermann Theater, named for the founder of the festival, on the right. Between the two lay a small plaza. It was in this open area that an hour's entertainment took place every afternoon and evening prior to each play in the Globe. Madrigals and other Renaissance music, skits, jugglers, and mimes got theatergoers in the mood for a little Shakespeare. I often could hear the entertainment from the tea room.

Tucked away behind a laurel hedge at the back of the complex was a squat, modern office building that housed all the people who worked behind the scenes to make the theaters work. It was in this hidden monstrosity that I hoped to find Kristof. I didn't know his last name, but how many Kristofs could there be?

I found the receptionist, a young, green-haired, gum-chewing woman sitting at a glass table in the middle of what looked like a waiting area.

"Excuse me. I'm looking for Kristof. I think he's a producer here."

Without looking up at me she asked, "Do you have an appointment?" Gum snaps.

"No. He was in my tea room the other day and he left a very generous tip for my waitress. I just wanted to personally thank him. You know, for being so supportive of the town's businesses." I hadn't thought of an excuse for seeing him before I arrived and that was the best I could come up with. But I was impressed with how easily the lies were slipping off my tongue lately. It had been a while since I'd used that particular talent.

"Huh. Well, okay. If you keep it really short I can let you back to his office. I saw him come in just a few minutes ago and I don't want you bugging him." She finally looked up at me and gave me a gimlet eye.

"No, of course not. I'll be very quick."

She gave me directions to the office and I made my way to it. The door was open, and the man I recognized as Kristof sat at a desk covered in scripts, drawings of sets, and several half-empty coffee cups. He was hunched over a schematic drawing of some sort. In his mid-forties, well dressed, with a head of thick blond hair, he wasn't an unattractive man. And if Gina was correct about him being a 'player' he must have known he was attractive and used it to his advantage.

"Hello?" I squeaked.

"Yes?"

Not looking up when greeting people must have been an office rule.

"I'm sorry to interrupt you, and I'll be just a minute. My name is Maggie O'Flynn, and you've been to my tea room a few times."

A quick glance up to confirm that I was indeed the woman from the tea room.

"Yeah, and?"

"Well, I was in the Garter the other night and heard how that dreadful Cressida Andrews was talking to you. She did

57

the same thing to someone I was with, and so I was just wondering if you knew what was bothering her that night." *Feeble, Maggie. So feeble.* I knew he would probably kick me out right then and there.

He glared at me over the tops of half-glasses. "Why would you care? And I think you should leave. The police have all the information they need about that night and I don't see why I should be talking to the tea girl about it." Nice. Tea Girl. "Go bother someone else. I don't have time for this." He blindly waved a hand in the general direction of the door.

Time for the near-truth. "Look. Do you know Nate Larimer from Friar's Book Shoppe? The police are questioning him and he's a good friend, and I'm sure they're questioning everyone else, like *you*, who was at the Garter the other night. I don't believe for a second that anyone here killed her, and I'm afraid the police, who've never had to investigate a murder in this sleepy little town, are going to try to hang it on someone here. Maybe you, even." Sorry, Rob. Under the bus.

He took off the glasses and sat them on the schematic. "While I agree that the police in this town are idiots, how is a tea girl going to help?" His eyes didn't stay on my face, but traveled down a short ways.

Before snapping back that I was no 'tea-girl' and that he needed to take his eyes off my breasts, I took a breath. "I believe that sometimes people just need to take things into their own hands. My previous job required excellent observational skills, and careful analysis of information." In a strictly theological sense. "Just thought I could bring that skill set to the people of this town and help people who I *know* didn't kill Cressida Andrews." I could see that the last sentence got to him. We were the same. We weren't killers.

Striking while the iron might be hot, I forged ahead. "What did Cressida have against you?" A better question would have been what did he have against her, but I would lose him if I were so direct. Hopefully we would get there this way.

A nasty laugh filled the small room. "I have asked myself that question a million times. That woman reviewed at least a dozen of my plays, and not once did she write a good review. Never." The words were spat out. "She hated every single one of them." He looked over his coffee cups and chose one to pick up and take a sip from. "Oh, she'd say some decent little thing about a set, or one of the minor characters, but everything else was always crap."

"How awful." I shook my head, commiserating. "But it seems like your plays do well, anyway. I was at *Much Ado About Nothing* last week and the Globe was packed."

"People figured out quick enough to ignore what she said." Another sip of cold coffee. "You like it? The play?" This time he allowed his eyes to roam the full five feet and seven inches of my body. I fought to hold back the shiver of revulsion I felt coming on.

"I liked it. Very much."

I stepped over to a large poster advertising a 2003 production of *Measure for Measure,* and looked it over. "So that argument I heard you two having at the Garter, with her calling you a hack, and you calling her a shrew, it was because of all the bad reviews?"

"Pretty much. Let's just say she won't be missed around here. By anyone."

Motive. Check. Opportunity though, I had no idea how to find that out. Unless…

Back at the desk, I rested both hands on it, leaned forward, and tilted my head to one side. "So, after the play tonight, you going out anywhere?"

This got me my first smile. "Perhaps."

"Where do you theater people hang out after the shows?" I asked in high flirtation mode.

"The bar at Tybalt's." Tybalt's was the town's posh restaurant. I had never been there but had heard that the bar was opulent. "Any chance I might see you there tonight, uh, Maggie?" Yes, you got it right. Maggie. Always good to know the name of the woman you are flirting with. I glanced down at his left hand and saw the wedding ring I knew would be there.

"Perhaps," I echoed his earlier answer.

I gave him my best seductive half-smile and turned and left, putting a bit of a sway in my hips.

Feeling like I needed a shower, I left the building and started toward the Garter.

Steve Talbott, owner and manager of the Garter Inn, was one of the first friends I made when I moved 'out west'. Not to say that I spent a lot of time drinking in the pub. But I quickly identified it as the place to meet the locals, and the hours I spent there did indeed introduce me to most of the citizenry of Stratford Upon Avondale. Plus, Steve was one of those kind souls who adopt people as others do stranded pets, and fathers them if needed. When I arrived in town I needed a little fathering. My own father had died a few years earlier, and my relationship with my mother had always been strained. Steve filled the parent niche very nicely.

It was still too early for him to be at the pub so I walked a few loops around the square, admiring the spring flowers before I went over and peered through the front window. I could see his stout figure behind the bar, making changes to the chalkboard list of specials for the day. My knock on the window brought him to the door with a wide smile on his face.

"Ah, Maggie! What a pleasure to see you so early in the morning. Come in, come in," he said waving me in to the still shadowy pub. Just like an authentic English pub the air was heavy with the smell of stale beer and last night's specials.

"Morning, Steve. I'm sorry to bother you so early, but I was wondering if you could help me with something." I worded it just right to appeal to his constant desire to help others.

"Of course. Come sit at the bar. Can I get you some coffee?"

"That would be great, thanks."

While he poured us two tall mugs of coffee, I asked, "How are you doing? How's Becky?" Becky was his wife of over thirty-

61

five years, the mother of their four grown children, and still the great love of his life. They were nothing less than inspirational.

"Very well, yes we're all doing well. Lizzie called last night and said she and some friends are going to Europe next month. She sounded so excited!" He laughed. Lizzie, at twenty-five, was his youngest and I always sensed a little favoritism there.

After hearing about Lizzie's trip plans, I delved into the matter at hand.

"The other night I was in the pub when Cressida Andrews was causing all kinds of problems, like picking arguments with several people." He nodded as I spoke. "There was one man, he was sitting near me, who had some words with Cressida. At first she was sitting with him, then she got up and went to the bar. He was a middle-aged, heavy-set man, wearing a suit and tie, though the suit was a little shabby. Any chance you know who I mean?"

He continued nodding. "Yep. Have known him for years. That would be Henry Russell. Been coming to Stratford for years. Poor guy. Life hasn't been so kind to him."

"He comes to see the plays?"

"Yeah, but as a reviewer, not a tourist. For years he was a critic for the Tribune, but I think that ended several years ago. Now he posts his reviews on some online theater blog, or something like that."

"Oh, that's kind of sad. Seems like that would be a big step down."

"It was. He's changed a lot since then, too. He used to be a friendly, outgoing man. The kind of person who would come into the pub, and be friends with everyone in the place by the time he left. Not anymore. Now he stays to himself." Steve's eyes glistened. The man had the biggest heart.

"Do you know if he's still in town? I'd like to chat with him if I could."

Steve looked suspicious, but didn't say anything. As the one person with his finger on the pulse of this town, he had to know about Nate, and it wasn't such a leap to guess what I was up to.

"Yeah, yeah, he's still here. He usually stays over at the Buckingham Economy, on Lysander Road."

I lifted the big mug with both hands wrapped around it and took a last sip of the coffee. "Thank you, Steve. I might try to see him."

"Maggie." He paused, looking me straight in the eyes. "Be careful. I can only guess what you're up to, but I worry it could be dangerous." More penetrating eyes. "And come to me if you need help. Okay?"

I stood and hugged him. "You're the best. I'll be careful, and you know I would come straight to you if I ever needed anything." Pulling back I smiled at my surrogate father. And the surrogate father to countless others in this town.

As I stepped through the door I turned and blew him a kiss.

I didn't want to talk to Henry before noon, thinking he would be sleeping off whatever his night's poison had been, so I found myself standing in front of Friar's Book Shoppe looking over the books displayed in the mullioned bay window, and wishing it were open. Or that I'd see a glimpse of its owner through the window. Or that he would come ambling up and throw his arms around me.

None of these scenarios came true, so I walked past my shop with the intention of heading to my apartment. The aroma of cakes and scones filled the air in front of the tea room. I'd rarely had the opportunity to be out front while we baked. The idea of passersby smelling hints of our freshly baked tea pastries made me smile.

Just as I passed the last shop on my stretch of Hamlet Loop—Viola's Sandwiches and Ice Cream Shoppe—, and was about to cross Juliet Lane, I saw the familiar figure I had just been dreaming about. Nate was coming up the street from the police station. He walked slowly, his head bowed, book in hand, intent on reading. I chuckled to myself—what a handsome-bookstore owner-devil he was.

As I neared him he looked up, startled, and shoved the paperback in his back pocket. "Maggie," he said the name like it was a song.

"Hey there, you."

For several beats we stood there on the sidewalk, silent, his discomfort palpable. "Yeah, so I was questioned again this morning." His eyes were now fixed on the sidewalk, little boy caught with his hand in the cookie jar.

"I heard. I hate that you're having to go through this." I reached out and took one large hand in mine, and squeezed it. I didn't let go.

He looked up from the sidewalk, and our eyes met. "I'm now officially Suspect Number One."

"No!" My free hand clenched, wanting to hit something. "That's ludicrous! They have no reason to think you could have anything to do with it. I mean—"

"Breathe, Maggie. It's okay. I'm confident they'll figure that out and that they might even find the real murderer. But it takes time."

He was far more calm and philosophical than I would have been. You would have thought *he* had been an ex-nun-in-training. If it were me I would have been having a fight with someone, or breaking something, or starting a brawl in the pub.

"But…an argument in the bar, some unanswered calls to your cell phone. That isn't enough to make you the prime suspect."

He looked out towards the square, and sucked in his lips. "Let it go, Maggie. We just have to be patient. I haven't been arrested." He laughed, a sound that felt as incongruous as laughter at a funeral. "I just have to 'not leave town.'" His fingers made air quotes.

"Really? Not leave town? Is this the wild west or something?" I shook my head and scowled into the bright sun. "Fine. You be patient. I'm going to be righteously indignant."

He reached out and touched my hair. "My fiery redhead." And his lips were on mine, my hand unclenched, and I moved closer to him until my body was pressed against his.

As pleasantly surprising as the kiss was, I pulled back and placed a hand on his chest. "Nope. You're not going to distract me with a kiss. Even an amazing one like that one. No. I'm sticking to righteous indignation."

"Okay. Go ahead. But no more investigating, Maggie. I mean it. That scares the bejeezus out of me."

"No worries there. I'm just heading over to Milford. Getting out of town and away from all of this for a few hours." Milford is the county seat. Where the county library resided. That place with all kinds of information, like old newspaper articles that I prayed would prove helpful.

"Now that sounds like a good idea. Enjoy." He smiled, and took off in the direction of our shops.

I admired his tall, lean form and broad shoulders as he crossed the street. Sighing, I turned and headed to my apartment and car.

"I'm afraid we haven't digitized everything yet, so those newspapers you want are still on microfiche," the librarian told me, handing me a box of the microfiche. She pointed me to the ancient microfiche readers that sat along a wall.

It took me an hour of mind-numbing and eye-straining searching before I located the first article I was looking for. It was written by Cressida five years earlier, and was a review of one of Kristof's plays. It was scathing. The only thing she seemed to like was the performance of one of the women who had a non-speaking role. She was especially harsh on the lack of creativity used in the design of the set.

Two other reviews of Kristof plays followed the same pattern. The last one I pulled up was only a few years old, and gave an exceptionally caustic review of one actor's performance whose name seemed familiar to me. Perhaps he was still in the company. In describing his performance she used terms such as "languid," "forgettable," and "the sex appeal of a newt." Certainly not the terms you'd want to read in regards to your performance as *Romeo*. I scribbled his name in my notebook: Jeffrey Lessard.

On a whim, I pulled out the six fiches that contained the paper's index of articles and editorials. On the third fiche I found the name I was looking for, and noted the reference number. Slipping the fiche into the machine my hand shook. Up and down the columns I scanned before finding it.

"Marooned Audience" the headline on the article shouted out. Such a surprise—she didn't like the Seattle Theater Company's production of *The Tempest*. But it was her review of one particular actor that interested me.

> *As if the Prospero debacle isn't enough to sink this production, Seattle gives us a wooden, dull Ferdinand. This actor is no Prince of Naples or any other kind of prince. I'm sure poor Miranda had a painful job trying to emote great love and passion for this Ferdinand as played by the talentless Nate Larimer.*

The sudden pain in my stomach quickly traveled to my chest as I struggled to get breath. Nate had been an actor. Was this the reason the police were focusing on Nate? And why hadn't he told me the truth? What else was he hiding? And worst of all, why had he acquiesced and gone out with Cressida, even if just for a beer, after she wrote this horrid review? I doubled checked the date of the review—it was six years old.

Something about Cressida's interest in Nate had starting niggling away in the back of my mind, leading me to look him up in the microfiche. While I'd suspected he'd had something to do with the theater world, I'd hoped I was wrong. I'd known it had to mean he'd come up against Cressida's cruel streak. Sadly, I was right.

Another check of the index showed no other reviews or articles that included Nate's name.

Nate Larimer had been an actor. And Cressida Andrews must have put an end to that career.

That's a strong motive for murder.

But Nate would never murder anyone.

He had opportunity. We parted plenty early that evening.

Nate would never murder anyone, I reminded myself. No. Not Nate.

He had means. At his height it would have been easy to hit Cressida over the head.

NO. Not Nate.

I took a much needed deep breath. Kristof had motive too. Opportunity was still in question.

This Jeffrey Lessard might have had a motive. I would check into him as soon as possible.

And there was still Henry Russell and that argument in the Garter.

Checking the time I saw it was after twelve. Time to get back to town and have a friendly chat with Mr. Russell.

~ five ~

A FTER PARKING DIRECTLY IN FRONT of the entrance to the Buckingham Economy Hotel, a miracle that warranted alerting the Vatican, I took a moment to text Gina to ask how things were going in the tea room. Her reply came quickly and was written in all caps. The gist of it was that I should go be a sleuth, though perhaps she worded it a bit more profanely.

As I walked into the lobby of the clean, functional, but unremarkable hotel it was with a much heavier heart than I'd left town with. The Nate situation had become more distressing with each mile I drove as I returned to town. I knew I needed to confront him, gently, but how and when were the big questions. It needed to be handled with care. The utmost care. This was Nate, my friend, my 'only in my dreams' lover. Kid gloves.

The problem was that I was not a kid gloves kind of person.

69

But first, there was Henry Russell.

The man at the front desk gave me Henry's room number without batting an eye, probably assuming I was a member of the oldest profession. Shaking that off, I took the elevator to the third floor and made my way down the carpeted hallway to room 318.

My knock was answered with, "Go away!"

"Mr. Russell, I have a delivery for you." Before leaving Milford I had stopped and bought an inexpensive fruit and candy gift basket, anticipating the need for some truth stretching.

Pressing my ear to the door, I could hear footsteps heading my way.

The door opened a crack. "Yeah?" Henry was dressed in gray sweatpants and an old blue T-shirt, frayed at the neck. I could smell the alcohol from where I stood.

"Good afternoon, Mr. Russell. I brought this gift basket for you, from the Stratford Upon Avondale Chamber of Commerce. It is to thank you for your continued commitment to our theater community." As I spoke I eased my way through the doorway, using the large, fruit-filled basket as my battering ram. "Allow me please to just set it there on your table."

He watched me place the basket on the table, a look of confused stupor on his face.

"Huh. Whatdya know? Kind of nice of 'em, huh?" He sniffed loudly and pulled the sweatpants up in the back.

"We hope you like it." Furrowing my brow, I peered at him. "Russell? Are you *Henry* Russell? You used to write for the Tribune, didn't you?" I sounded like I'd just met a celebrity, I gushed so enthusiastically.

Nodding, he said, "Why as a matter a' fact, I am. I am that Henry Russell." He squared his shoulders. Or at least he attempted to.

"I always read your reviews. They were the only ones I trusted."

"Yeah. I usually got it right, didn't I. And without any of that holier-than-whose-it stuff that some critics use. All the nasty stuff, *some* critics think makes them sound smarter than everyone else." He swayed as he spoke.

"Well, I've missed your reviews. Why did you leave the Tribune?"

"A witch on a broom flew into town and took my job right out from under me. This witch didn't know the first thing about theater or anything." As he spit out the words, actual spittle sprayed into the air.

"Oh, no. That witch wouldn't have been Cressida Andrews would it?"

He sat down on the edge of the bed, presumably because the room was spinning too much for him.

"God dang woman!"

Shaking my head, I said, "I couldn't read her reviews, they were always so mean."

"She's dead, you know." There was a glint of glee in his eye.

"I heard. You know, I saw her just hours before she died. She came into my tea room."

"Good riddance, I say."

"It is a little scary thinking that someone murdered her. I mean, I could have been outside at that same time, and it could have been me!"

He laughed. "Couldn't have been me. I spent that night with my friend, Jameson."

"Who's Jameson?"

He got up off the bed, stumbled over to the mini-kitchen, picked up a bottle from the counter, and returned holding up the almost empty bottle of Jameson Whiskey. This seemed to tickle him, for he started guffawing, which quickly turned into loud coughing.

"Well, I'm so glad you're safe. I need to get going now. I hope you enjoy your basket." I was out the door before he could even register that I was leaving.

Henry Russell was a sad, pitiable man. He also was a man with an excellent motive for murder. Though he could have been lying about his whereabouts at the time of the murder, I tended to believe him. Of course he was drunk that night. So it could have been possible he acted in a drunken stupor with no memory of it. I mentally put a question mark next to his name.

The tea room was packed at one o'clock when I returned, and I could see the looks of relief on the three women's faces as I walked into the room. Julie hadn't been able to come in. I pulled my weight for the next three hours, but my mind was far from the tea room.

After we closed up I shared everything I'd learned with

Gina, who stayed late just for that purpose. She was as stunned as I was to learn about Nate's secret past.

"Who would have guessed? I mean, he's gorgeous, of course, would make a dang handsome actor, but it's just hard imagining him up on a stage," Gina said.

We both fell silent, staring into space. I knew I was imagining the handsome Nate treading the boards, and I was fairly certain Gina's thoughts were much the same.

Bringing myself back to the task at hand, I broke our reverie. "What do you think about Kristof? Motive, yes. Opportunity, maybe, but not sure."

"We could go to Tybalt's tonight and ask some of the actors there if Kristof shows up every night after the play."

I slowly nodded. "Yeah. Yeah, that's what I had been thinking, too."

"And that Henry guy, he sure has a good motive, but do you think he could have staggered down to the river and bumped off Cressida?" Gina asked.

"Not likely. But I wouldn't eliminate him yet."

Casey had come back into the dining room while Gina and I were discussing Henry. She stood next to our table, wringing her hands. "Now, I don't want this to come out sounding wrong, but if you didn't know Nate, and he wasn't your friend, don't you think you'd suspect him? He's got the motive and the opportunity. Means too I'd guess." She spoke with her face all scrunched up, fearing retaliation most likely.

All afternoon I had been trying like the devil not to go there. On top of everything else, he hadn't told me about the acting and the review, and probably hadn't shared it with the police either. It didn't look good, that was for sure.

Gina jumped up from her chair, blessedly changing the subject. "Hey, I forgot to tell you. Something came for you today." From under the register she pulled out an envelope and handed it to me. *Maggie* was all that was written on the front. The handwriting was decidedly masculine.

I opened it to find two tickets to that evening's performance of *Othello*. I stared at them, thinking, for several seconds before turning back to Gina.

"So, you want to be my date for a little Shakespeare tonight?" I asked Gina. "Then we can go on to the gathering at Tybalt's."

"Why did you get two hand-delivered tickets?" Casey asked, eyes narrowed with suspicion.

"I'm guessing it was Kristof. Part of his seduction plans I'm sure." I shuddered a bit at the thought.

"Or…" Gina said dramatically. "They're to throw you off the scent and make you forget about his possible involvement in a murder!"

I shrugged. "Either way, my friend, I think you and I have a date night."

Feeling badly that Casey was being left out, I turned to her and said, "Do you want to meet up with us at Tybalt's? Make it a real girls night out?"

"Nah. Wish I could. But Rob's been gone so much with this murder that I've hardly seen him the past couple of days. He promised to be home tonight so I should probably be there too."

I patted her hand. "We'll miss you, but that's the right choice. Plus, if we discover anything I can text you and you can get info from Rob."

Her face lightened at that. "Yeah, that sounds like a plan!"

"Great. Thank you, Casey. Gina, I'll meet you in front of the theater just a little before curtain, say seven-twenty for the seven-thirty curtain?"

We finalized our plans and I started home to glam myself up a bit. After all, I had a role to play at Tybalt's if I was to get the information I needed.

The seats Kristof had arranged for us were in the top deck of the Globe, one of only two areas of the small theater that boasted actual modern day theater-style seats. The rest of the circular theater had benches, though unlike in Shakespeare's time these had backs to them for today's more picky audiences. The main floor, however, was just as it would have been in the bard's time—standing room only. Where the 'groundlings' stood to watch the plays. This area seemed to attract the younger, more rowdy theatergoers. Again, just like in Will's time.

The fact that I'd seen this play just a week before didn't lessen my enjoyment of it a second time. I did have a fondness for Shakespeare, but if I was completely honest my enjoyment of this particular production had more to do with the gorgeous actor in the lead role. The one I saw at the pub the night of Cressida's murder. His deep voice as it spoke

Shakespeare's elegant words did things to me, and I sat mesmerized for three hours. A few glances at Gina during the production told me he was having the same effect on her. Perhaps it was her mouth hanging open every time he was on stage that tipped me off.

As we filed out of the theater into the dark night, she whispered, "I wonder if that Othello will be at the bar tonight?" She cackled.

I sighed. "One can only hope."

Tybalt's was a mere few steps from the theater, just on the other side of the stairs that led down to the park and river. We would be there long before any theater company folks could possibly arrive.

Four months I'd been in Stratford Upon Avondale and I'd never stepped foot in the town's most elegant restaurant. As we entered it I got little more than a glance at the dining room, which appeared to be softly lit, and plush. The bar was immediately to the right as we came in, and as my eyes lit on that room I knew the elegant dining room could never compete. A cross between old Hollywood and a Nineteenth Century British men's club, the room was overflowing with opulent red tufted seats at the booths, mirrors on every wall, crystal chandeliers, intimate tables with wing-back chairs, and candles burning everywhere. The bar itself was a long, highly polished wooden affair, behind which stood three bartenders dressed in tuxedoes. It was after eleven, so there were few people still in the room.

It was the perfect setting for a group of Shakespearean actors to unwind.

Gina and I stepped up to the bar and sat on stools right in the center. I had brought out the Secret Weapon for tonight's sleuthing, and Gina was in the micro skirt she'd been wearing on Tuesday. Her clinging top was cut exceptionally low, and she had plenty to fill it out. We both wore shoes with heels we could barely balance on. I ordered a dirty martini, and Gina asked for Bourbon on the rocks.

Nursing the drinks, we waited nervously for the group to come in. What we would do once they arrived neither of us knew. Perhaps I could ask one of the cast members if Kristof was always there till the bitter end of the night. I shared this idea with Gina.

She laughed. "Hmm, I have my program right here," she said pulling it out of her tiny purse. "Let's see who you might want to strike up a conversation with." Her tone held a strong teasing note.

I grabbed the program from her hands. "Don't be a fool. Any one of these actors would do the trick." But my eyes went straight to the dotted line that led from the character, *Othello*. Darius Thulani. I turned to the bio section and read that Mr. Thulani was from London, England, the son of Nigerian immigrants. He studied at London's College of Dramatic Arts. This was his first production in Stratford Upon Avondale.

And, I hoped, not his last.

Just as we were giving up hope of anyone ever arriving, a group of five cast and crew members walked in. They were soon followed by a larger group, and finally just minutes later a still larger group of people. The room quickly filled with the sounds of men and women who were off of work and ready for their own happy hour.

Peering at the mirror behind the bar, I checked my lipstick and fluffed my hair, gathering it over to one shoulder, a look I always thought was sexy. I was zapped by sudden guilt that I was in some way cheating on Nate, but reassured myself that Nate didn't seem to be in any hurry to commit to a romantic relationship. Besides, I was only here to gather information that would prove Nate's innocence.

I was saying something to Gina when I felt a hand on my back. "Well, how nice to see you here, Maggie," Kristof oozed.

Wanting desperately to shake that hand off, I turned to face him. "And thank *you* for the tickets. We enjoyed the play very much." I rested a hand on Gina's shoulder. "Kristof, this is my friend, Gina."

After his eyes took her in from top to bottom, he said, "My pleasure. Nice to meet you, Gina. Can I get you ladies another round?" His hand never left the small of my back. The spot itched so much it started to burn.

I answered for both of us, "Yes, thanks."

He gave us each a smarmy smile, and said, "Of course. And let me know if there's anything else you need." His eyes rested on Gina's chest.

After instructing the bartender, he stepped away, for which I was immensely grateful. Our drinks appeared quickly, as if the bartender was accustomed to taking good care of the friends of Kristof.

"Follow me," I whispered to Gina and slid off my stool. With my martini glass in hand I waded into the throng.

I eyed the assemblage, looking for a face, any face, I had not seen, or at least not noticed, on the stage that evening. It wouldn't matter if it was someone on the crew, or someone with a small non-speaking role I wouldn't have taken note of. All that mattered was it had to be someone no one would notice talking to the two women strangers.

As my eyes wandered the room, they happened upon the dark eyes of one Mr. Darius Thulani, who was looking directly at me. I let my eyes rest on his and smiled crookedly at him before looking away. Probably not the smartest move to have made at that moment, since I had now been noticed, but I simply couldn't help myself. At least the Secret Weapon was working in this room.

But then I saw her. A lone woman, standing near the back of the room, glass of white wine in one hand. With Gina in tow I made my way across the room to her.

"Hi," I ineptly began. "My first time here. My friend and I were just wondering who all these people are. When we got here it was so quiet. Do you know?"

"Oh yeah. We're from the theater. Kind of our habit to come over here to blow off some steam after a play."

Gina picked it up. "Really? Wow. Are you an actor?" she gushed. Well done, Gina. I wanted to give her a high-five.

"Kind of. I work crew, but have done some acting in smaller theaters. I'm hoping to act here some day." Her head bobbed up and down and back and forth as she spoke, as if to music only she could hear.

"That's cool." Gina said, still playing the role of adoring theater fan.

"You know, I think I know that man over there," I said pointing to Kristof as he was flirting with the pretty woman who had just played Desdemona. "He's been into my shop. Isn't he a producer or director or something?"

After a sip of wine, she answered, "Producer." Bobbing.

"Oh yeah. So even the producers come to this every night?"

"They would never miss it." There was a surly hint of sarcasm in the answer.

"Yeah, but look at him with that woman. I'll bet he doesn't stay to the end when everyone else leaves, does he, if you know what I mean." Wink wink.

"Him? No way. He's usually out of here with some pathetic woman as soon as he can get her drunk enough to agree." Her disdain for the man and the women who fell for his lines came through loud and clear.

"Oh my god! I think I saw him on Tuesday night. About midnight, in the square. He was with some girl, being all grabby."

"Tuesday night? Hmm, I think he stayed pretty late that night. No, I don't think it could have been him." The girl's eyes wandered away from me, scanning the room for any of her theater mates—my time obviously having run out.

Dang.

I didn't have long to wallow in my disappointment, for Othello stepped up next to me. The air crackled with the electricity sparking off his body.

"It seems I keep seeing you across crowded rooms." That voice! All on its own, I thought, it could probably impregnate me.

Catching my breath, I muttered, "Seems like it." I looked into the darkest eyes I'd ever seen. They were like deep lakes at midnight, the bottom of which you could never quite see.

"I'm Darius."

Damn, what is my name? Maddie? Molly? "Maggie," I announced a little too loudly, pointing to myself. And then remembering my manners, I pointed to Gina, "And my friend, uh, Gina."

"Nice to meet you finally, Maggie. And Gina." As he spoke, one brow cocked upward. You'd think after that performance he would smell like stale sweat but instead he had a manly, musky scent that was much more appealing.

"Your Othello was mesmerizing," I managed to say, though I didn't remembering thinking it before it was coming out of my mouth.

With a small bow, he said, "Thank you. It's a role every actor dreams of, and I was very fortunate to be given the opportunity."

Gorgeous. Sexy. And gracious. Wow. What a trifecta.

I saw out of the corner of my eye that our crew member had moved away and was now chatting with a skinny young man with full sleeve tattoos covering both arms.

Still in a stunned state with Darius so near, I was thankful when Gina took over. "So you guys hang out here after every production?" She was giving him a come-hither smile. I knew exactly what thoughts were going through her head, and if I could've I would have slapped her back into reality.

"Most nights. Not everyone, but most of us," The Voice said. Looking at me now he asked, "You two thinking of becoming our groupies?" One corner of his mouth went up in a sexy smirk that should have been outlawed for the damage it could do to the morals of all womankind.

Finding my own voice I said, "No, probably not. This was just a girls' night out kind of thing."

"You visitors to Stratford, or live here?"

"We both live here." My how bold I was getting. "I own the Merry Wives Tea Room, and Gina works with me there." I stopped short of drawing him a map to the shop.

He leaned forward from the waist, hands in his pockets, a bemused smile on his lips. "You make your tea the proper English way?"

"You better believe it! I'm kind of a snob about tea. No bad tea served in my tearoom!"

"Well next time I'm feeling homesick and need a good cuppa I'll know where to find it." His eyes bored into mine and I couldn't help but pick up the possible double meaning.

Gina's hand grabbed my arm. "Well, Maggie, I think we need to get going. It was great to meet you, Darius." She tugged on my arm, trying to force me to move. I shot her a look of incredulity. I couldn't believe she was willing to leave the presence of Darius. I knew I wasn't keen on leaving him.

Begrudgingly, I said, "Yeah, you're right. Glad I finally got to meet the man I keep seeing in crowded rooms." I extended my hand and it was grasped by a large, strong, warm hand. "Perhaps I'll see you when you're thirsty for tea."

"Perhaps." How could one word carry with it so many layers of meaning? "Good-night, Maggie." Somehow that deep voice went even deeper as he said my name.

I smiled at him and reluctantly released his hand as Gina pulled me away and toward the door.

Once we were outside, she said, "Pull yourself together, girl!" We both giggled. "But, wow. Just wow."

"Wow, wow, wow, wow," I said through laughter. "And who's telling who to pull themselves together, huh? You were practically drooling. I think you'd already named all the children you two would have and had moved onto planning the grandchildren!"

"But seriously now, I thought of something while *you* were planning how many babies *you're* going to have with Darius. Look," she pointed to the stairs that led to the riverside park.

"Yeah, so?"

"That girl said she thought Kristof was there till the end on Tuesday, but she didn't sound so sure. And did you see how crowded that room was? Kristof could easily have slipped out and been down in the park, even clear at the other end, in just a few minutes if he ran. Killed Cressida and been back up here before anyone noticed he'd left."

I peered down the stairs and considered this. It would have been possible. And if I was right about Cressida watching from one of the B and B windows for someone to show up on the path, Kristof would certainly be someone she would willingly meet. They might have even had something going on, since Kristof seemed to have little regard for the ring on his finger and what it stood for, and Cressida 'collected men' in Nate's words. The two actually deserved one another.

"You know, I think you're on to something there," I told Gina and then explained my thoughts.

"I think Kristof just moved up on our list of suspects," she said. "I mean, really, how convenient that he was so close to the path at the time of the murder. Probably closer than anyone else on the list of possible suspects."

"Good point. Proximity is a big factor."

Motive: lousy reviews. Opportunity: looking promising. Means: sure, why not?

We were standing in the shadows at the top of the stairs, when a man I recognized from the cast came out with an attractive young woman. When the woman turned her head I realized it was Courtney, from the Garter. They were arguing, and though it seemed they were trying to keep their voices down, I could hear most of what they were saying.

"I told you it was over. A long time ago. Damn, it's been a year!" the actor said.

"Just the fact that you were *ever* with that woman is too disgusting."

He let out a low groan. "For the hundredth time, I didn't sleep with her because I liked her. It was all about what she could do for me *professionally*. I didn't want to be another one of those actors whose careers was ruined by Cressida. It was like an insurance policy, I swear."

"Well lucky for you she's dead now, huh? I can only imagine what she might have written about you this season since you refused to have sex with her anymore."

Gina and I grabbed each other's arms.

"Guess we'll never know," he snarled. "Hopefully, she

would have been a professional about it and written the truth. That I do a great job in my role." He laughed, but it was a tension-releasing laugh rather than one of mirth.

"I've got to get home and get some sleep," Courtney said sharply, shaking her head. She started walking toward the square.

"Fine," he snapped. "But promise me we can meet for dinner tomorrow." The Globe produced their plays on alternating days, so on that day it had been a tragedy, *Othello*, and the next day would be the comedy. Meaning the actor would be free the next day.

Over her shoulder she said, "I'll think about it. Let you know tomorrow," and she picked up her pace and cut across the square.

The actor watched her walk away, and when she was safely out of ear shot, growled, "Damn it!" before heading back into the bar.

"Oh. My. God," Gina said. "We've got another suspect!"

We moved over to a streetlight and I opened the play program. "I think he was Roderigo. Let's see," I moved my finger down the list of characters. "Jeffrey Lessard."

It took a moment before it hit me.

"I saw that name today in an old review! Cressida said awful things about him and his acting."

"Maybe after the review he struck up a deal with Cressida and arranged a little quid pro quo, if you know what I mean," Gina said, wagging a finger back and forth.

"And this week she got mad that it wasn't happening this year, which in turn angered him, and he killed her. Good lord, Gina, if he was in the bar on Tuesday he would have had just as easy of a time getting to the park as we thought Kristof would have had."

"And," she picked it up there, "she would have met him thinking he'd changed his mind and it was time for her booty call! I'm sure there was no way she would have missed that opportunity."

We stared at one another, sharing in a feeling of exhilaration that we might very well have solved the murder.

"I need to text Casey and tell her to let Rob know our suspicions. This seems like a serious possibility."

"Yeah, but you've got to make sure she makes it sounds like we just happened upon it," Gina pointed out.

"Of course. And she can say that I mentioned something about the bad review because I was just looking up stuff about Cressida. Make it all seem really casual."

Gina nodded furiously. "Yep, yep, that should work. Oh my god, Maggie, I think we did it. I think it has to be him."

Before we parted I dashed off a text to Casey explaining what we discovered and what we inferred from it, and asked her to mention it to Rob. I added a bit about making it sound casual and that we just happened upon the information. She texted back immediately and assured me she would talk to Rob as soon as she ended the text.

Turning back to Gina, I said, "I'll see you in the morning. Hopefully there will be some news about Jeffrey."

Looking like a petulant child, Gina stood with her hands firmly placed on her hips.

"I need disco fries," she grumbled.

"And just what language are you speaking?" I asked.

"Jersey. After a late night, especially if you're drinking a lot, which of course we didn't do tonight, but still…disco fries would sober you up if you had been drinking a lot, and oh my god they're so good." She stared out into the night sky, seeing something other than black sky.

I let out my breath in a loud burst. "Okay. Tell me what they are. I know you're not going home until you do. So it sounds like something you can only get in New Jersey, right?"

"Damn straight. Most diners served 'em. At least in my corner of the state. First you have fries, the big kind, you know, steak fries. Then over that they pour cheese sauce. Then over that they pour chicken gravy. Well, I guess some people prefer brown gravy, but I only ever had them with the chicken gravy." She licked her lips. "So good. And all that fat and grease bonded with the alcohol or something and sobered you right up. A late night ritual where I'm from."

To my ear it sounded like a heart attack on a plate, but I grimaced and said, "Yum yum. So sorry we don't have them here. Maybe you could try making them yourself some time."

"Uh, who wants to be doing all that cooking in the wee hours of the morning?"

Silly me, I should have known better.

"Just stop thinking about them, now. Let's go home. We'll talk in the morning if there's news about Jeffrey."

Nate, we might just have what we need to put an end to your nightmare.

~ six ~

Friday, May 22nd

W*HO NEEDS MORE THAN THREE hours of sleep?* I
asked myself as my alarm clock went off at five.
I had an hour and a half before I had to deliver
scones to Ruth Williams, so turning off the alarm and going
back to sleep wasn't an option.

I grabbed my phone off the nightstand to check for any new
texts from Casey. The last I'd heard before going to sleep was that
Rob planned to tell his superior about what we had heard. His hope
was that he and another officer would question Lessard first thing
that morning. Casey's texts had sounded positive and upbeat.

When I pulled up new texts there were none from Casey,
but I did find two from Nate he'd sent in the last twenty
minutes. The first asked for me to text him when I could,
and the second was inviting me to meet him for coffee.

I replied that I could meet him at The Mustard Seed, a
small cafe on the other side of his bookstore, at seven. His
'see you then' was immediate.

In the previous twenty-four hours so much had happened I hadn't even had time to decide which parts I'd share with Nate. The only thing I knew for sure was a confrontation was in order—he had some explaining to do when it came to the deep, dark secret of his acting past. The rest was going to require great care in disseminating. I didn't need Nate thinking I was playing Jessica Fletcher.

Ruth Williams, an African-American woman in her mid-sixties, along with her retired husband, Leo, ran the Anne Hathaway's Cottage Bed and Breakfast. While the Lady Grey was housed in an old mansion and commanded a million dollar view, Anne Hathaway's had a more quaint and inviting atmosphere. Stepping into the living room felt like coming home. Much of that was due to the warm and friendly Ruth, and the mood she set at her B and B.

She greeted me with a megawatt smile, and a hug.

"Good morning, Maggie May," she sang. I had no idea how I became Maggie May, but she'd taken to calling me that shortly after we first met. It stuck, and I rather liked the ring of it.

I walked into her comfortable living room and the mouth-watering aromas of breakfast sausage, freshly baked bread, something maple, and brewing coffee teased me. Rumor had it Ruth served the best breakfasts in town.

"Hi, Ruth. Sorry I'm a little late. My bad. I was out late last night." I was sure I didn't need to tell her that—my red eyes and the dark circles under them told the story.

"Oh now, none of that. You know I'm flexible about little things like that. We just love your scones enough to wait all day if need be." Her laugh sounded like it bubbled up straight from her heart.

Feeling the need to confess my sleuthing ways to someone besides my partners in crime, I whispered, "Yeah, but, Ruth, I was out trying to find evidence that someone other than Nate Larimer killed Cressida Andrews." I bared my teeth in a grimace and raised my brows nearly to my hairline.

"Oh my. Now why would you be doing a thing like that?"

"Nate's a good friend, and well, I'm not sure the police are trying all that hard to find other suspects."

"You're not kidding? They actually suspect Nate?" She sounded incredulous.

"Yes. And of course he had nothing to do with it."

With a look of consternation, she said, "Of course he didn't. That man is salt of the earth." She made a humph sound and folded her arms over her chest.

Leo walked in and waved at me. "Hey, Maggie. I'll take that box from you. Think I'll nab one for myself before I put them out for our guests." He waggled his brow, teasing.

Handing over the box, I said, "Leo, I was thinking. Someday when we both have time, could we talk about a website for my tea room?" Leo had retired from the tech industry and when not helping with the running of the B and B he'd been building websites for some of the merchants in the village.

"Sure. Be a pleasure. Why don't you think about the kind of information you want on it, and when we sit down we can start to draw up some ideas."

"Okay, sure. Thanks so much, Leo."

After he left us alone again, Ruth whispered, "I don't know if I like the idea of you trying to do the police's work. It could be dangerous," she said emphatically.

I looked into her concerned, caring face and for a moment wished my mother could have been more like Ruth Williams. Ruth was everything my mother was not.

"I promise to be careful. And all I'm doing is keeping my ears and eyes open, really," I said, trying to reassure her.

"Well, all right. Don't need to hear about something happening to you."

I gave her a big hug. "Nothing bad is going to happen to me. I'll be here tomorrow morning just like always. And the morning after, and the morning after."

We both giggled as I let myself out.

For someone like Ruth Williams, early morning deliveries were never a bother, but an anticipated pleasure.

As I opened the door to the Mustard Seed, the aroma of coffee was like a shot of adrenaline to my exhausted body. I stumbled toward the counter with visions of caffeine soon coursing through my veins. I knew I looked a fright, with dark circles under red eyes and I hated the idea that Nate would see me like this. But I didn't want this chat to wait.

Once I had my coffee, I collapsed in a chair at a table

tucked away in a corner. Both of my hands circled the mug of hot coffee, my face just inches from it as I hunched over the elixir. When Nate came through the door we acknowledged one another with a quick wave and he made his way to the line to order. I hoped I was wrong, but he didn't look too happy.

When he sat down across from me with his coffee and breakfast sandwich I was on number seven of my mental practice rounds of what I wanted to say. And even after seven tries I still wasn't sure how I was going to approach any of it with him.

"Hey," he greeted me. There was no smile, and he looked almost as tired as I felt.

"Hey, yourself."

"You kind of went AWOL yesterday, after I saw you." He stirred some sugar into his cup of coffee, the task taking his full attention. "I checked by the tea room a few times, and no Maggie." More stirring.

"I told you I went into Milford. Kind of got into it and just lost track of time." I knew he suspected I was still looking into the murder, but I had to deflect those suspicions.

"Oh."

Heading the rest of it off at the pass, I said, "And last night Gina and I had a girl's night out. Went to *Othello* and over to Tybalt's for a little while."

He nodded. "Good. That sounds fun."

"Well…it was." I decided to take advantage of the natural segue. "We overheard something that might indicate that someone other than Nate Larimer murdered Cressida."

I smiled and nodded, encouragingly. *See Nate, good news.*

"What? Were you doing your Jessica Fletcher imitation again?" His eyes narrowed with suspicion.

"No, it was totally a case of the right place at the right time. I can't tell you more yet, but I think the police will be questioning someone first thing this morning."

Any residual anger left his face and his body slumped inward, visibly relieved.

"I'm more than willing to share the spotlight with anyone else who would like it," he said, a hint of the old Nate in his voice.

"Both Gina and I think this questioning will lead to the real murderer being arrested. I'd be surprised if we didn't hear something by this evening." I grinned at him. He let his eyes linger on my face, a smile playing at the corners of his mouth. I leaned over the table, and placed my lips on his. Neither of us moved for what felt like hours.

When the kiss ended I questioned myself on whether or not I wanted to bring up what I had discovered about his past. I decided to wait. At least for a few minutes.

Nate told me he wouldn't be at the shop all day, as he had a carpentry job to take care of. It was at a local winery and the thought of him building something with his hands in a romantic setting like a winery sent my mind to fantasy land.

"Maybe we could go there together some time and do some wine-tasting," I suggested.

This brought a smile to his face. "Now, that's the best idea I've heard in ages." He picked up my hand and raised it to his lips.

I took a deep breath after the oh-so-romantic-hand-kiss, and dove right in. "Um, Nate, yesterday, you know, while I was in Milford, I went to the county library. I thought I'd read some of those awful reviews by Cressida that everyone's been talking about." Oops. Did he know everyone was talking about the reviews? Or was that just people *talking to me* about the awful reviews? Fortunately he didn't react to it.

"I ended up reading a few years worth," and to add comic relief I said, "on old microfiche, can you believe it?" I laughed, but even to my ears it sounded false.

"I saw one for a theater in Seattle," I paused, gauging his reaction to the city name. His eyes that had been admiring his cup of coffee were now on me. Narrowed eyes.

"*The Tempest.* Cressida didn't like it much."

"Nor did she like an actor named Nate Larimer, right?"

I pressed my lips together and nodded.

"I'm surprised you never told me," I said. "That's a big part of your life that you've never mentioned. You know about my nun-in-training years, I would have thought you would have taken that opportunity to share your own sordid past." I said 'sordid' with big, round eyes, making sure he knew sarcasm was to be indicated.

The fingers on his right hand started strumming on the table. It went on for a long minute while we both were silent, me holding my breath.

When I was ready to give up any hope of him ever uttering another word, he smirked. "So, what you're saying, is that you don't have anything else in your *sordid* past to tell me about?"

Uh-oh.

There might have been. But how he would know about it I couldn't imagine. As far as I knew, no one else in the town, or even in any of the western states, knew about that.

"You're turning a little pink in the cheeks, Maggie." Oh my god, he was enjoying torturing me. That smirk.

"If, and I'm just saying *if*, you had something else you hadn't told me, I'm sure there would have been a good reason, right?" He should have worked for the CIA. His skills at torture would be very welcome there.

I peered at him through squinty eyes.

He continued, "Like you were saying earlier, sometimes people just happen upon things." *Please make this end.* "Maybe I happened upon something, too." *Damn that smirky voice. What a tease.*

Don't make me say it, Nate. Please. That would be death by embarrassment. No. Just spit it out, because there is no way I'm saying it.

"Could I have happened upon something? *Cassandra*?"

I threw my head on the table, my hands, clenched, on each side of my head.

"Oh wait, what's this I have in my back pocket? Oh yes, that book I was reading." He was holding back a laugh that obviously wasn't going to stay in much longer.

Oh, dear Lord, just put me out of my misery now.

"Hmmm, written by Cassandra St. Jean. On the cover a bare-chested man is trying to rip that bodice off that buxom blonde. On the inside back cover, an author picture of an attractive redhead. I should probably tell you I've already read the first two in this series."

I decided before I died I might as well have one more glance at Nate, so I peeked out from under my hair. Looking down at me, he touched an index finger to his tongue, removed it and pretended to be touching it to something. "Tttzzzzzz…" he made a sizzling sound with his mouth.

Staying right where I was, I whined, "All right. Yes. I'm Cassandra St. Jean. I write steamy romances."

"Steamy?" The laugh finally got to escape. "That's what you call them? I'd go with sizzling hot."

I sat up, threw my hair out of my face. "They are not. They're just steamy. They aren't…" I lowered my voice, "erotica. There's actual guidelines for these things, and mine are termed 'steamy.'"

"If you say so, Cassandra. Or can I call you Cassie, since we're friends and all?" More loud, man laughter. I glanced around at the tables near us, and caught several sets of eyes aimed in our direction.

"You're mean. That's just mean. The fact that I write romances, and do so under a pen name isn't something I feel the world needs to know. Hence the pen name!"

The smile he gave me right then made me forget any anger I might have felt. We sat silently, with him smiling an adorable closed lip smile at me. When neither of us could hold it in any longer we both laughed out loud—I'm sure making us the cafe's center of attention again.

After using a napkin to wipe the tears off my face, I leaned across the table and asked, "Can you answer one question for me?"

"I suppose."

"If you've been reading my books, and you know I'm no nun, why have you been so hesitant about, uh…making a move?"

It was time for his face to redden.

"Maggie, there was no way that I, a normal real-life male, could live up to what the men in your books are capable of."

Looking up at him from under my lashes, I said in my best breathy voice, "First, I know reality from fantasy. And second, you should let me be the judge of your…capabilities, Mr. Larimer."

Word travels quickly in towns as small as Stratford Upon Avondale. By noon rumors were flying about the handsome actor who was a suspect in Cressida's murder, and my tea room was packed with residents and visitors alike who wanted to share what they knew. No arrest had been made, but according to Casey, Jeffrey Lessard was questioned for nearly three hours before they let him go.

"What I don't understand is why they let him go," Mrs. Phillips, a regular customer, said.

Casey, who was hovering near the table, spoke up. "They have to check some of the stuff he told them. You know, alibis and things like that."

Ruth Williams sat at Mrs. Phillips' table and said, "I hope they're keeping an eye on him. We don't need a murderer wandering around loose in the village." She looked my way, giving me a warning eye.

"I'm sure they are," Casey reassured her.

Lucy Garcia, a waitress from the Robin Goodfellow pub, added, "I heard he had an affair with the murder victim." She sat at a table filled with local residents. Sarah Vachon, Jane Morris, and Jenny Schneider who worked at the bakery, all sat with Lucy.

"Where did you hear that?" I asked her, wondering how that information got out. I knew neither Casey or Gina or I had said anything.

"Just around, you know. It sounds like a lot of people knew about it." Both Sarah and Jane, the oldest women sitting at that table, wore looks of disgust and disapproval on their faces.

Sarah shook her head. "Young people these days."

"Cressida was no young thing," I reminded her. "And she was very much a part of it."

"No, but he is, and I can't imagine why he would have wanted to be with that woman!" Sarah's face puckered like she'd just bitten into a sour pickle.

Jane joined her in shaking her head, looking like she was about to be ill.

"I'll admit the thought of it is pretty disgusting," Jenny, who was about my age, piped up. She'd been unusually quiet up to that point. "But what people do in their private lives shouldn't be any concern to anyone else."

"I couldn't agree more," a vaguely familiar masculine voice said. I turned to find myself looking into the face of Kristof, who had come in unnoticed. He gave me a look that made me feel itchy.

"I'm afraid I don't have a table at the moment, but if you can wait ten minutes or so, I'm sure something will be opening up."

Gina pushed her way in front of me. "What awful news about that actor," she said. "Did you have any idea that he…and Cressida…?" She finished the thought by angling her head severely to one side.

He glanced at Gina and looked back at me. "No, no. I don't get involved in my actors' private lives. Look, I was just stopping by to ask if you enjoyed yourself last night, Maggie. And you too…I've forgotten your name," he said looking at Gina. Without waiting to find out her name he continued, "I didn't see you leave the bar." *No, we were busy discussing how you could have killed Cressida.* And if it turned out Jeffrey couldn't have done it, I still thought Kristof made a viable suspect.

"The play was wonderful, and *Gina* and I had a nice time at the bar. Thank you for the tickets."

He tilted his head, and openly gazed at certain points on my body. "I hope to see you at the theater or at Tybalt's again soon."

Though he was staring at me, Gina stepped up and said, "Maybe we'll do it again. Uh, Maggie, Laura was asking if you could help in the kitchen for a little while."

Thank you, my savior. I nodded a good-bye to Kristof, and hurried away to the kitchen. Just seconds behind me, Gina came through the door, too.

"I still think he might be the murderer," she announced. "He's just slimy enough to murder someone with his bare hands." She shuddered.

"I couldn't agree more," I said. "Maybe if things turn out that Jeffrey is innocent, then we should tell Rob our suspicions about Kristof."

"Yeah, maybe. Have we eliminated that other critic, what was his name?"

"Henry." I paused, giving it consideration. "I don't know. I think he has the best motive of all of them, losing his job to her. But I don't think he would have been out along the river at that hour. I'm pretty sure he would have been passed out cold in his hotel room." With his friend, Jameson, I silently added to myself.

Gina agreed and rushed back out to the busy room. I took over the order Laura was working on and sent her back out as well. I was in no hurry to listen to any more murder talk.

I was sure that closing time would never arrive. After my three hours of sleep the night before, and an intense day in the tea room, I was feeling a bit like a murder victim myself. Needing a break from murders, suspects, sleuthing, and romantic frustration, I said goodnight to Casey and Laura and strolled down to the theater complex to watch the pre-play show. The Friday play in the Globe was a comedy so I knew the pre-show would have the same tone. I watched a little of it and the music and bawdy comedy skits refreshed me and distracted me from reality.

When the show was over, I went over to the Garter for a quick beer and to say hello to Steve. I made my way to the bar, hoping for an empty stool, and saw a welcome face sitting there. Nate. By some miracle the seat to his right was open and I grabbed it.

"Hey there," I greeted him.

The enormous smile on his face told me he was just as pleased to see me, as I was to see him. "Hello…" I liked the way he said that one word, like it had implications.

Before we had a chance to say anything more, Steve came over and said, "Hi, Maggie dear. So, yesterday, did you—"

"Yes! Absolutely. You were right, that's a much easier way to get to Milford. Thanks so much for the help." He stared at me, blinked twice in confusion, and slowly nodded his head.

"Good, good," he stammered. "What can I get you?"

"Whatever IPA you have on draft, please."

After Steve turned away to get my beer, I looked over at Nate. "So, I was just wondering," I began, then paused, took a deep breath, and plowed forward. "How did you happen upon my books, anyway?"

"I own a bookstore, Maggie." Smirky, sarcastic Nate was much sexier than he should have been.

"I know that. But of all the hundreds of books you carry, what made you look at the inside cover of a *romance*?"

We were interrupted by Steve bearing beer. I avoided his eye, and thanked him. Not until he was busy with another customer did Nate and I continue.

"One day I sold four copies of your books, different titles, but all these Cassandra St. Jean books and it made me wonder what they were, and why they were suddenly so popular. I read the back blurb and opened to the back inside page and there you were, smiling at me. I wouldn't have been human if I hadn't been intrigued and wanted to find out what my friend was writing."

I ran my fingers through my hair, pushing it back off my face. "I know there's nothing I can do to rewind time, but you gotta know this is pretty embarrassing for me, right?"

"Nothing to be embarrassed about. They aren't what I normally read, but they're good. Well-written. Good plots and characters. Kept me reading, and now I'm on my third." We each took long swallows of our beers.

"Well, thank you, I guess. So, do you ever wish you were still acting?"

He grabbed a pretzel and ate it before answering. "Sometimes. I'm very happy with my life right now, but I would be lying if I said I didn't sometimes get that bug to tread the boards again."

"Ever thought of trying out for one of the county's little regional theaters, you know to just get yourself started again? I'm sure they would be thrilled to have an actual professional actor!"

"It's crossed my mind, but I'm worried I'd be pretty damned rusty after all these years.'

"Hmm. You should think about it some more."

We finished our beers and chatted while managing not to mention the murder or investigation.

When we were both finished, I told Nate I was exhausted and needed to get home, eat something and get to bed early.

"Why don't you let me buy you dinner here? One less

thing for you to worry about. Then I'll walk you home, make sure you find your way in your exhausted state. We could take the river walk, and enjoy the sunset over the river." He raised one brow and waited expectantly for my verdict.

"Sure, that sounds very nice actually. Thank you."

I managed to stay awake while I ate a steaming bowl of beef stew. We ate leisurely, as he told me about his acting days and I shared a little about writing romances.

Later, when we got up to leave I took a page from Cassandra St. Jean. Rather than waiting for him to reach out to me, I simply took his hand and held it in mine, and we walked out the door together.

From the stairs I could see the riverside park was much quieter than I'd ever seen it at this hour. Very few people walked along the path, fewer still sat on the strategically placed benches. As we turned and started down the pathway it was as if we had this bit of heaven to ourselves. The setting sun cast a golden glow over the trees on the far bank and added glittering amber highlights to the dark water.

Nate released my hand and placed his arm around my shoulders, while guiding me to the water's edge where we stopped to admire the scene.

"'Kissing with golden face the meadows green, Gilding pale streams with heavenly alchemy'." Nate's deep voice spoke barely above a whisper.

"That's beautiful, and so absolutely perfect for this," I

said, also in a whisper, like someone would use in church.

"Shakespeare. A sonnet. Though I think it was about sunrise, not sunset. Still the words fit this scene like the man was here himself."

Nate the strong carpenter/bookstore owner could quote Shakespearean sonnets. Impressive and so very attractive. I snuggled closer to him and wrapped my arm around his waist. He was warm and I could feel the muscles in his back.

In silence we watched the sun disappear behind the hills on the other side of the river, until all hints of the gold that colored the landscape had been swallowed up by the coming twilight.

As the landscape lights came on to greet that twilight we turned back to the path and continued walking, arms still around one another.

Our silence was comfortable, companionable and where I would normally feel the need to fill that silence I allowed myself to enjoy the quiet, listening to the sounds of the water rushing over rocks, and the noises of the night.

Without warning, Nate stopped and spun me to face him. His hands moved to my face, cupping it in those strong hands. Our eyes met before he bent to kiss me. Soft, gentle, warm, the kiss carried a promise of passion. When he broke the kiss that promise left me breathless.

On legs that were now wobbly, I held Nate's hand as we continued along the pathway. The sky to the west still held light while to the east it was becoming increasingly violet. But there was still enough light to enjoy the view of the water as it made its way past us.

We came around a bend in the pathway, a bend required by a massive boulder that jutted out of the river onto the sandy riverbank. As we cleared the boulder I felt Nate tense, and a microsecond later I let out a short, sharp scream, leapt back, and fell backwards onto my butt.

A man's body lay face down on the riverbank, legs on the sand, torso and head in the water. Even in the gathering darkness I could see the red stain on the boulder, just above where his body lay.

I sat on the bench next to Nate, a blanket from Casey wrapped around us, and a paper cup of hot tea clutched in my still shaking hands. For the past two hours we had been sitting on this bench just outside of the crime scene tape as the forensic team did their job and sheriff detectives sporadically asked us questions. Though the sheriff had been involved with the first murder investigation, now that there were two murders the case had been handed off to the county sheriff's department and their more vast resources. Rob and his cohorts were now relegated to 'helping' as needed. I suspected this disappointed Casey much more than it did Rob.

As I took a sip of the blessedly hot tea, Rob stepped over the yellow crime scene tape and came over to us.

"We have a preliminary I.D." He paused, whether for dramatic effect like they do on every TV crime drama, or to watch us for signs of shock I didn't know. Finally, when we didn't have any reaction of any kind, he continued. "It looks like it's that actor Jeffrey Lessard. The one we were just questioning this morning." Morning felt like weeks ago. And Lessard? But he had to have been the murderer of Cressida, so he couldn't be a victim. That was impossible.

"Are you sure he was murdered? Could it have been an accident?" I asked. Nate's arm tightened around me, drawing me closer to his side.

"It could have been an accident, but since it looks so much like the Andrews murder we're going to treat it as suspicious."

"Could it be a copycat?" I knew I was grasping at straws, but I didn't want my perfect solution to the first murder to be torn to shreds.

"While anything is possible, it is very unlikely to be a copycat."

"But you said earlier that he died after his head hit the boulder and then fell into the water and drowned. So that means that, if it was murder, it wasn't exactly like the other one. So it could be a copycat," I argued.

Rob took a long breath and let it out slowly. "No, not really. Copycats generally *copy* the fine details of the other murder. Hence the name 'copycat.'"

I knew that. Of course I did. And Rob was just being a smart aleck. But I was a desperate sleuth who didn't want her first solution to turn out to be wrong. Also, if Jeffrey wasn't the murderer, could they still suspect Nate?

Nate must have been thinking along lines that were parallel to mine, for he asked, "Any idea what time he was killed?" Nate had been with me since a little after six-thirty.

"The pathologist thinks he's been dead about four or five hours, so around five o'clock, maybe. I wouldn't want to be quoted on that."

That timeline was not good news. I was at the pre-play show at five-fifteen or so and I had no idea where Nate was at that time. My mind went to Kristof. Where was he at five o'clock?

"Five o'clock? How is it then that we were the first people to find the body? Weren't there plenty of people down here at that time?" I asked, my voice high and squeaky.

"The park was closed between four and six, for mosquito spraying," Rob answered.

"I thought they did that later, more in the evening hours," Nate said.

Rob nodded. "Normally they do, yeah. Tonight the guy who does the spraying had some family thing he had to go to later, and decided to take care of it early."

A closed park meant Jeffrey and the murderer snuck in past the closure barriers, which in turn meant they had to have planned the meet up or entered the park together.

"You two can go now, but we might have more questions for you tomorrow. Go home. Get some sleep."

Sleep. That's all I had wanted since I stumbled out of bed at five that morning.

"Let me get you home," Nate said softly as if I were a nervous mare.

"Home sounds like heaven."

After handing the blanket to Rob to return to Casey, Nate and I backtracked to the other end of the park since the crime scene blocked our way to the entrance that was only 100 feet away. We each kept an arm tightly wrapped around the other as we hurried out of the park.

We made it all the way to my apartment without saying a word, each lost in our own thoughts. I unlocked the outer door and waved Nate in. He didn't protest.

At my door I fumbled trying to get the key in the lock and eventually dropped it on the floor. Nate bent to pick it up, and without trouble got the door unlocked on the first try. We stepped into the dark flat. I found the lamp and turned it on as fast as I could, nearly knocking it over in my haste to get some light in the room.

"You should take a long, hot shower and get right to bed."

I nodded mutely and started to hobble across the room to my bedroom. Before I got to it I stopped and turned to look at Nate.

"Would you mind sleeping on my couch tonight? I really don't relish the thought of being alone here tonight."

He gave me a lazy, tired smile. "Of course. Actually, I was going to suggest it myself. Throw me a blanket and I'll be quite comfy on your couch."

I went to the linen closet and got him two blankets and a towel, and then went to my room to get a pillow off my bed.

Back in the living room I handed them to him. He caught me by the shoulders, pulled me close and kissed me on the cheek.

"Get some sleep now," he told me. "Good-night. And

sweet dreams." The way he said sweet dreams made me think that despite everything that had happened I probably would have sweet dreams of his voice saying those words.

"Good night," I said. "And thank you."

I staggered back to my room and closed the door.

~ seven ~

Saturday, May 23rd

THE SOUND OF THE ALARM awakened me at six—having set it an hour later than normal when I had crawled into bed—but my brain remained foggy and confused and unable to figure out how to make the piercing sound stop. My defense was to crawl deeper under the covers and hope to muffle the annoying sound that way. When my bedroom door opened a few seconds later it terrified me. I was bewildered that someone seemed to be in my room. It wasn't until the familiar voice said, "Maggie?" that some of the pieces of the puzzle started to slip into place.

Nate.

He had spent the night on the couch.

I had been afraid to be alone.

And this was because we had found the body of a murder victim.

Click. Click. Click. Each fact found its place in the puzzle.

I hazarded a peek, pulling the covers down a half an inch. Nate stood at the foot of my bed, shirtless, wearing his jeans, looking exactly like a cowboy on the cover of a romance novel.

"Nate?" My voice, froggy, cracked on the one syllable.

He turned off the alarm.

"Yep, it's just me. Sorry to come in, but when the alarm didn't go off I got a little concerned. Everything okay?"

"It will be. Woke up kind of confused. Wasn't sure what was going on."

I sat up, holding the covers pulled up to my neck.

"I know the feeling. Did you get much sleep?"

When I had closed the bedroom door that night I couldn't believe I had Nate spending the night in my apartment and that I had no desire whatsoever to attack him. Murder is quite the mood killer, as it turns out. But knowing he was out there I had doubted I was going to be able to sleep. That only lasted thirty seconds before the exhaustion got me and I was sound asleep.

"I can't believe it, but yeah I did. I slept like the dea…uh, I slept like a rock."

"Good. If it's okay with you I'm going to start some coffee, or tea if you'd prefer, and will meet you in the kitchen whenever you're ready."

"You're a real sweetheart, Nate Larimer. Thanks. I'll be out in a minute."

Not the way I'd envisioned our first breakfast after a sleepover, but it didn't matter because I was just happy to have his company.

When I got to the kitchen, bathrobe cinched tight, the aroma of coffee hit me. I saw he also had the electric kettle heating in case I wanted tea. He was placing slices of bread in the toaster and had butter, peanut butter, and jam on the counter. A girl could get used to this kind of treatment.

I stepped up behind him and put my arms around his waist, resting my chest and head on his back. "Thank you, Nate," I said into the fabric of his shirt. "For everything. Staying. Breakfast. Basically taking care of me. You're pretty wonderful."

He turned around in my arms and placed a kiss on my forehead.

"My pleasure. Completely. Absolutely."

"How're you feeling this morning? Get any sleep, after all that…you know, last night?"

"Your couch was great, but, yeah, there were a few images I had a hard time getting out of my mind."

The toaster popped up our toast, and I let him loose to take care of it for us.

With our coffee and toast we sat down at my table before he popped the bubble we were briefly living in.

"I got a text from Rob before you came out. Seems the fact that I found the body puts me back on top of the suspect list."

I spoke with a mouth full of toast and peanut butter. "What? How can they think that? I don't understand." Frustration and a mouth full of toast made the words come out in sharp bursts of sound.

"I don't think Rob thinks I did anything. But he said it's general policy to suspect the person who finds the body. Of course you did too, but you weren't already a suspect, so you get a pass. Not me. I have two strikes against me now."

"Look, I know you would prefer me not doing the Jessica Fletcher thing, but don't you think if I do a little investigating it could help?" I didn't wait for an answer before adding, "Gina and I thought it was Jeffrey, based on that conversation we heard, and obviously we were wrong. But we also saw some stuff at the bar that same night, that could indicate that Kristof Lewis, the producer, is the murderer." Not the full truth, but most of the truth.

"Maggie…" He tipped his head to the side and gave me a glare out of the corner of his eye.

"But listen," I interrupted. "If Kristof murdered Cressida, and there's reasons he might have, and let's say Jeffrey found out about it then he would have had motive to also kill Jeffrey. Don't you think it's interesting that both murder victims are connected to the theater and Shakespeare festival in some way?" I was thinking out loud. I hadn't put those pieces together until that moment, but it rang true and was definitely possible.

"I'll agree it sounds possible. But if it is possible then I'm sure the police will figure it out, too."

I nodded, but simply to end the discussion. I had no intention of ending my own investigation. In the mystery books and TV shows, whenever a second murder was committed it was because the sleuths were close to the truth. I was sure that was the case in these murders as well.

I needed to talk to Gina, but couldn't as long as Nate was in my home.

How crazy was I that I wanted him to leave?

With an awkward kiss good-bye, as if we were kids who were caught spending the night together, Nate and I went our separate ways at seven-fifteen. A deep fog had settled into the village overnight, leaving everything in its path damp and cold. It was into this miserably depressing grayness that I hurried over to Hathaway's Cottage to apologize profusely to Ruth for not making my usual delivery. When she heard the reason behind my absence she was both shocked and forgiving.

"What is becoming of our lovely village?" she asked. "Two murders in just a few days." She shook her head. "And that poor young man. So awful." She looked near to tears.

I hadn't thought about it, but of course the murder of Jeffrey would bring a greater sense of grief to the town than that of the universally disliked Cressida. Jeffrey was a member of the community, and well known to most of the town. Plus he was likely to be beloved by his fellow company members. Ruth's reaction to the news would be how many citizens of Stratford Upon Avondale would also react. It was a good reminder to me to proceed gently and with care as I tried to find the killer and prove Nate innocent.

And poor Courtney. I thought I might stop by the Garter at some point in the day and ask Steve how she was doing with this tragedy. She saw Jeffrey just before he was killed and, as I knew only too well, they hadn't parted on the best note.

After leaving the B and B I texted Gina and asked when she could meet me. Her reply came seconds later. She reminded me that she was at the tea room—starting at seven, of course— and since we wouldn't open for another two hours or so, we'd have plenty of time to discuss things there while we prepped for the day. Feeling foolish that I'd forgotten Gina worked for me, and recognizing the fact that I still wasn't firing on all cylinders, I gave myself a mental head slap.

I picked up my pace and hurried to the tea room.

Gina and I reviewed our case while preparing the teacakes, scones, and tea sandwich fillings. Some of the more specialty items would have to wait until later, if we made them at all that day.

"Casey texted me and said Rob says they might question Kristof some more. It doesn't sound like they gave him much thought the first time through. I don't think they knew about the reviews," I told Gina.

"See, that's where amateur sleuths come in handy," Gina shouted.

"Exactly! I wish everyone recognized that fact," I said, thinking of Mr. Larimer. It wasn't as if I saw myself as a reincarnation of the *fictional* Miss Marple.

"On the other hand though, I'm not really sure," I admitted. "The fact that we were so sure it was Jeffrey and then this happened has me more than a little frustrated. Maybe we don't know what we're doing after all."

"Now, none of that," she barked. "Oh my god, I sound just like my mom!" Gina rolled her eyes.

"I wonder if there's some way we could talk to Courtney. I know she's probably in shock and is grieving, but she probably knows more than most anyone else about Jeffrey and what he's been up to." I froze, then slapped my floured hand to my forehead, leaving flour all over my face. "Courtney!" I cried. "She told me on Tuesday night that Cressida was an old friend of her mother's. I think she mentioned something about college friends, which means they really were old friends."

Gina and I stared at one another, and it was a testament to the speed at which our brains were operating that she didn't laugh at the way I looked, covered in flour.

She broke the heavy silence. "It seems like a pretty gigantic coincidence that Courtney's boyfriend had an affair with a woman Courtney's mother knew."

"And, don't you think Courtney herself must have known Cressida too? I know my mother's oldest friends," I said.

Gina slowly, deliberately nodded. "Yep. Yep. She must have. Did you say she was there in the pub during all those arguments Cressida got into?"

"Yeah." It was more of a question, as I wondered where she was going with it.

"So she saw it all too, and yet I don't think we've heard anything said about her being questioned. First, she saw the actions that led up to the murder. Second, she probably knew Cressida. If I were a detective, I'd want to question her."

"Me too. But I think that's impossible right now. I'm certainly not going to bother her. I'm sure the detectives already are. Someone had to tell them that Courtney knew Jeffrey." We fell silent again, until I had a thought. "What we need is someone who knows her well, who could maybe give us a little information."

"Yes, that's good. But who?"

"Steve Talbott would probably know a lot about her. She works for him, and isn't she one of his adopted strays, too?"

Gina's eyes lit up. "Yes! We should talk to him!"

Giving great attention to the scones I was making I said, in a low voice, "I don't think I can. I've gone to that well already this week, and he kind of had to lie for me the other day. I don't think he'd like to talk to me about Courtney." I turned to look at Gina, my eyes pleading with her.

"Sure, I'll do it. I'm really starting to feel this detective thing going on." She grunted as she iced a small teacake with little finesse. The wretched thing looked like a melted candle—one that had burned unevenly.

"You have to make it seem perfectly casual, like it's something that just comes up in conversation," I reminded her.

"I know exactly how to handle it. He'll never guess I'm after information for our case."

"Why don't you plan on going over there after Laura gets here."

"Sure."

When I'd been walking over to Ruth's B and B, I'd had another idea, too. It would be very helpful if I could see

117

Cressida's room and check to see if it did indeed have a view of the path. Another visit to the overly-grief-stricken Jane Morris seemed in order.

When I told Gina what I was thinking, she agreed and we made a plan that as soon as she returned from the Garter, I'd head over to the Lady Grey.

While Gina was out I called Julie to come give us a hand. Saturdays were always our busiest day and with Gina and me taking turns leaving the shop I knew we'd need more help.

It was getting close to noon, and still no Gina. She'd been gone for over an hour and a half. With everything going on in this town, I started to get worried.

I was just about to run over to the Garter to check on her when she blew in through the front door, her eyes wide as she tried to silently communicate something to me. I took it to be good news, that she had indeed been successful in getting information from Steve.

As I untied my apron I quietly let Laura know I'd be out for a short while. Before leaving I stopped in the kitchen for my purse, and made sure that both my phone and a pad of paper and pen were somewhere in its depths. Locating everything needed, I left for the Lady Grey.

A smiling Jane Morris answered my knock on this visit. She beamed when she saw me, as if I was her lifelong best friend.

"Maggie," she sang. "How good to see you again." She

showed me in and we went into the Room of Photographs.

We exchanged our pleasantries before I delved into my pack of lies.

"Jane, I was wondering if you could help me. I have some family coming to visit next month and my little flat just doesn't have enough room to put them up. It's my aunt and uncle. I was hoping you might have a room available that they could book."

"Oh, sure, sure." In these words I heard, for the first time, an upper mid-west accent, as if she came from Minnesota or North Dakota.

"Just come into my office and I'll check what's available."

I followed her in, and was met with another wall of photographs. Like the ones in the front parlor, these too were of Jane and various guests.

"I'm hoping for the third weekend of June. And if not the weekend, even mid-week would be okay." I didn't want to be turned away, or I'd never get to move to the next part of the plan.

She put on half-glasses and peered at a computer screen.

"You're in luck. I have a very nice room open that weekend, at the back of the house."

"Oh, that sounds lovely. I'll bet it has a view, right?"

Jane smiled proudly. "Why, yes it does. Quite a stunning one, if I do say so myself."

"I hate to be such a bother, but my aunt is rather picky about things. Do you think I could see a room, one like the one you have available, if there's one that's free at the moment?"

"Well, as a matter of fact, room three is between guests and I think it's been cleaned and is ready for occupancy. Would you like to see it?"

"Does it have the view over the river?"

"It does," she puffed up like a smug peacock.

"I really appreciate you allowing me to see it."

She grabbed the key from a cupboard full of sets of keys, and led me upstairs.

As we passed room two, she whispered, "That was Cressida's room. Always room two." Jane bowed her head.

"Oh my," I said, unsure what the proper response should be. "Have the police allowed you to start renting it out again?"

She stiffened. "I can't let anyone else stay in that room! The police are gone, no crime tape or anything, but it just seems wrong to let someone else sleep in her bed."

I let it go, but with plans to return to the topic after I saw room three.

She unlocked the door and opened it for us. I went in, and gushed over the beauty of the room, knowing she would expect it. An abundance of lace and floral patterns seemed to be the decorative theme.

I slowly made my way to the window, carefully making sure Jane saw me admire the duvet on the bed, the flowers on the dresser, and the paintings on the walls.

Looking out at the park below I was pleased to see the room had a commanding view of much of the pathway. I could see where Cressida's body had been found as well as where Nate and I found Jeffrey's. Of course it had been dark at the time in question and I worried the view would have been greatly limited at that time. However, the landscape lamps might have cast just enough light for Cressida to make out a familiar figure.

"How lovely, I know my aunt would be very impressed with a view like this and a room so perfectly appointed." I smiled to myself—I was becoming quite the adept liar.

Directing my attention to a small rectangular table along the wall, Jane said, "And as you see each guest or couple is given a gift basket when they arrive. I like to fill them with things that are representative of Stratford Upon Avondale." She oozed pride.

"What a nice touch."

"Yes. Of course Cressida's baskets were always very special. I'm afraid I always got carried away trying to make each one better than the year before!" She giggled, sounding like a schoolgirl.

The mention of Cressida was perfectly timed.

Conspiratorially, I leaned close to Jane and asked, "I know it's asking far too much, but I was wondering if I could take a peek at Cressida's room. You've made me feel like I missed out by not getting to know her."

Jane looked at me for several long seconds, clearly considering whether I was worthy enough to step inside the great Cressida's room.

"All right. But I ask that you please not touch anything." Her face was drawn, pained.

"Oh, of course not." I gently laid a hand on her arm to indicate my understanding of the shrine I was about to enter.

We left room three. She locked it up and went next door, where she stood before the door, eyes closed as if in prayer.

Just when I was sure she had changed her mind, she opened her eyes, placed the key in the lock and led me into the holy room.

Much like the room next door, this room had a queen bed covered in a floral duvet, an antique dresser, prints of flowers hanging on the walls, and lacy curtains at the window that looked out over the river. I stepped to the window and saw the same clear view of the path I'd seen next door.

"Quite lovely," I said appreciatively.

Before Jane could reply, a woman carrying a tote filled with cleaning supplies stopped in the doorway.

"Jane," she said, "could you come to room seven for a minute?"

Jane looked flustered and unsure of what to do with me while she was away from the room, so I quickly said, "I promise to just stand here and enjoy the beauty of this room without disturbing anything." I gave her a broad smile to reassure her.

Looking from the cleaning woman and back to me several times, she finally nodded in my direction and left for room seven.

I knew the room had been thoroughly searched by the police, but I still had a flicker of hope some clue could have been left behind that would lead me to who she had met that night. Having seen the view of the path I was more convinced than ever that she had watched for the person from this window.

Thinking of every mystery I'd ever read or watched on TV, my eyes scanned the room, looking for places something could be hidden. A door leading to what I assumed was the bathroom caught my eye and I went over and opened it quietly. An immaculate bathroom was all I could see. I turned back to the room and noticed a book sitting on a low shelf on one of the nightstands. Quietly hurrying over to it, I picked up the book. It had a floral cover with the words 'Guest Book' embossed in elegant script on the front cover. Surely the police would have seen the book, but with some unwarranted hope I flipped to the last pages.

> *May 15*
> *Thank you, Jane, for the usual lovely room. Just as with every visit I feel like I've been dropped into a floral nightmare. And this time you really overdid it with the gift basket. How many cheap Shakespearean souvenirs do you think I need?*

Surely Jane had seen this. How could she remain so devoted to such a cruel woman?

Some scribbles at the bottom of the page caught my eye. Written on a diagonal as if scratched down quickly, I saw four numbers. They were stacked for adding, and came to a total of 4,597 if Cressida had done her math correctly. I assumed it was Cressida's math since the pen used seemed to be the same one used for the vicious note. The ink was purple. The pen attached to the guest book had a design on it that matched the cover—I quickly pulled it out and wrote a line on the palm of my hand. Black ink. I opened the drawer on the nightstand. No pens. I decided I could safely assume Cressida had written the numbers, whatever they meant. Voices approached the room. I stood straight as if admiring the view.

"I'm sorry we had to be interrupted, Maggie. Are you ready to book that room?" She held her hands in front of her chest, tightly clasped together.

"I think they will love it, but let me just call them tonight and double check their dates and tell them about the room. I'll let you know as soon as possible."

As we walked down the stairs she nodded her approval.

"Oh, Jane, I was wondering if Cressida's family has plans for a service. I haven't heard anything."

"Yes, but back in Kansas, where she was from."

"I'd like to send a card, maybe some flowers. Do you happen to know Cressida's favorite color?"

She laughed. "Oh my yes. It was purple. I always had a bouquet of purple flowers in her room whenever she stayed here."

"How sweet and attentive of you."

She smiled a timid, self-deprecating smile, and shrugged.

We reached the front door. "I'll stop by or call you when I have an answer from my aunt and uncle. Thank you so much for showing me the room."

"My pleasure. We'll talk soon, then."

It wasn't until I was out in the fresh May air that it occurred to me that for the last half-hour I'd been inhaling the heavy scent of potpourri. Jane must have had it, or an oil perhaps, stashed throughout the house. I breathed deeply, clearing the irritating fragrance from my lungs.

The afternoon was turning very pleasant, with temperatures edging into the seventies and the sun beaming out between fluffy white clouds. The morning had been so damp and dreary with fog I had given up on a nice day. Now I felt my step quicken with the energy that always came when the sun shone.

Or perhaps with the excitement of a sleuthing job that's gone well.

Gina and I didn't have any free time to share our findings until an hour after the shop was closed up for the day. Casey stayed as well.

Before turning our attention to the case, Gina asked, "You doin' anything fun tonight? Maybe something with a certain sexy-demon bookstore owner?"

"I don't think so. Actually I haven't seen him since early this morning."

I hadn't. Not passing by the window. Not stopping in for a tea to go. Remembering what he said about the text from Rob, my heart threw in several extra beats.

I turned to Casey. "Have you heard anything from Rob today? Did they question Nate anymore?"

"No, I haven't talked to him since I came in."

"I hope that no news really does mean good news."

"I can text Rob if you want."

"No, don't bother him. Maybe after we all compare notes

I'll go next door and see if Nate's there."

I went over to the register and got a piece of paper and a pen before sitting at one of the tables, where Casey and Gina joined me. After scribbling down the number I found in Cressida's guest book I asked Gina what she'd learned.

She sighed. "That Steve is such a sweetheart. Dang, he's got the biggest heart in the world. First, I found out he really watches out for Courtney and worries about her like a father. How sweet is that? And because he watches out for her he's seen some things that could be helpful." I guess I looked alarmed because she quickly added, "Don't worry. I was super casual, he thought we were just having a friendly chat. Really. Totally fell for it. Anyway, he knows about Courtney's mom and Cressida being old friends. Oh, and he told me Courtney's mom lives in Colorado.

"Is Courtney from Colorado?"

"Yeah, that's what Steve said. I think she's been out here for maybe four or five years. About as long as me."

"I wonder what brought her out here?" Casey asked.

"I don't know," Gina said dismissively. "Colorado isn't the point of this story!" She scowled at Casey and me. "He said that every time Cressida was in town she would look for Courtney. But things got weird, according to Steve, about two years ago."

Casey and I sat quietly waiting for her to continue, afraid to say anything. Gina glared at us, as if daring us to interrupt again. "So, starting a couple of years ago he would see them talk to one another, and Cressida always looked upset about something. And this time was the worst. He said that

Cressida came into the pub on Monday before it opened and took Courtney out front, you know so Steve wouldn't be able to hear. But they stood in front of the window and he said Cressida looked angry and kept pointing her finger in Courtney's face and even poked her in the chest a few times."

"What does he think it was about?"

"He doesn't know, but I'll tell you, if that had happened back home in Jersey, it would have meant Cressida was shaking Courtney down. You don't go around poking people in the chest unless you've got something on 'em. Just sayin'." She flung both hands out, palms up, to illustrate just how obvious she thought the situation was.

She picked up her Garter report where she'd left off before her editorial digression. "And I could tell Steve wished he did know. It was almost like…and I don't think I'm imagining it…it was almost like he's worried Courtney had something to do with the murder." She'd lowered her voice as if someone could have heard her in the empty room.

I tapped the pen on the table and stared out the window. If Cressida was angry at Courtney about something and Courtney didn't like it, would that be enough to make her murder Cressida? That seemed like a giant stretch. However, if Courtney was also upset with her boyfriend and the nauseating knowledge that he had slept with Cressida numerous times to keep her from writing any more bad reviews, then she might just have reason to want her gone. Permanently gone.

I explained my thinking to Gina and Casey.

When I finished Casey said, "I agree that it gives her

reason to kill Cressida, though I just have a really hard time imagining her hurting anyone. But where I think it goes off the rails is when you think that it means she must've have killed Jeffrey, too. I just don't see Courtney doing that." She shook her head. Of the three of us, Casey was by far the most empathetic.

"But Gina and I did see that argument they had on Thursday, just before he was killed. They say anyone can commit murder given the right circumstances."

"They do?" Casey asked.

"I don't know. It sounded good. I think I've heard it in a mystery, or something," I said.

Gina nodded sagely. "It's true. Anyone can kill. Take my word for it." Both Casey and I eyed her warily.

"They did argue…" Gina said, returning to the topic at hand. "She was freakin' angry and disgusted by the Cressida thing. But by then Cressida was dead and no longer a threat to their relationship."

I put my head in my hands, elbows resting on the table. "I don't know. This is all making my head feel like it's going to explode."

Gina stood. "Why don't I make us some tea, and maybe get a few teacakes for us, then you can tell me about your trip to the B and B."

"I'll give you a hand," Casey said.

They scurried off to the kitchen to make the tea. It was so true, tea is the answer to all life's problems. I laughed to myself. It certainly was presented as the cure for everything from a broken leg to a broken heart in every English TV show I ever watched. Everyone was always putting the kettle on.

Casey was right about one thing. It was hard to imagine sweet Courtney hurting anyone, let alone murdering someone.

Over aromatic cups of Darjeeling and tangy, moist lemon teacakes I told them about my visit to the Lady Grey. When I got to the part about the window and the view of the path Casey slapped her hand on the table.

"I keep forgetting to tell you! That night, on Tuesday, it was a full moon! Remember how it was a clear day? Well, it was a clear night too, and I remember it being a full moon that night." She smiled wryly. "Rob and I had a romantic moment that was brought on by looking at the moon." She took a sip of tea, unable to make eye contact with me.

Gina rolled her eyes and said, "TMI girlfriend! No one needs to know *why* you know it was a full moon."

"So if Cressida was watching for someone from her room she'd have had a perfect, well-lit view of the path," I said, ignoring Gina's outburst.

"Yes!"

"At least that's one thing we can check off. Cressida probably *did* watch for whoever she was meeting, and that person killed her." I took a bite of the cake before returning to my reporting. "Okay, I found one other thing," I said. "Her room at the B and B had a guest book, and Cressida's entry was the last in the book." I went on to explain about the numbers and the purple ink and how I was sure she had written the numbers.

"What do you think they mean?" Gina asked.

"No idea. Yet. The entry, and probably the numbers, were dated Monday." I wasn't sure why that would be important but it felt like it should be.

"And Monday was when Cressida and Courtney had their big argument," Gina added.

I nodded slowly, mulling it over.

Casey looked at the clock and exclaimed, "Oh yikes. It's later than I thought. I told Rob I'd have a great, home-cooked meal ready for him if he could get himself home at a decent hour. I haven't even been to the store." She stood and ran to the kitchen to get her things. When she returned, she said, "You get next door and see that hunky bookstore owner. If I hear anything from Rob I'll text you."

In a blur the little pixie woman was out the door. Gina followed her out a few minutes later. I locked the door behind them and went to the kitchen to finish up a few things before taking Casey's advice and visiting the bookstore.

I just prayed Nate was there and not a guest of the county.

~ eight ~

Sunday, May 24th

I STEPPED THROUGH THE ARCHED doorway of the church into the drizzle of a gray Sunday morning. The sunny days of the past week were unusual for May, I was told by long-time residents. I wanted them back.

Sadly, the gray, dismal morning fit my mood. While I'd been relieved to find Nate at the bookshop the evening before, I'd also been disappointed when he turned down my offer of dinner out, on me. When I suggested a quick pint at the pub, he hemmed and hawed and made up some excuse about being tired and just wanting to go home and sit in front of the TV.

I knew he felt disconsolate about being back at the top of the list of suspects. Most likely his dismissal of me was only due to that. But I couldn't help but wonder if it really was me. I was starting to think his concern about living up to my male characters was simply an excuse to avoid hurting my feelings. Whatever the case might have been, I knew when someone was putting the brakes on a possible relationship, and it felt an awfully lot like Nate Larimer was putting the brakes on us.

As I got into my car for the return trip home from St. Lawrence's in Milford, my phone pinged. Casey. All the text said was *Big news. Meet me. 11:00 Mustard Seed.* I noticed it was a group message, and she'd included Gina in it as well.

Merry Wives didn't open until one o'clock on Sundays, giving me plenty of time to meet with Casey. Glancing at the car's clock I realized I needed to hurry to get back to town in time.

Driving out of the parking lot, I wondered just what Casey thought constituted being called 'big news.'

None of the three of us had what could be called a quiet voice, so it was with great deliberation that Gina, Casey, and I kept our voices low as we sat hunched toward one another at the little table in the Mustard Seed.

"The investigators got a call from Cressida's attorney in San Francisco this morning," Casey reported. "About her will. Sounds like Cressida was a wealthy woman, and she left some money to Courtney." To make up for the inability to shout this information, Casey's eyes were open so wide I could see the whites entirely circling her irises. Her eyebrows shot nearly to her hairline.

I was still processing this information when Gina grabbed my wrist on the table and whispered, "Motive!" Even her whispers were gravelly.

"Do you think she even knew about being in the will?" I asked. "And would it have been enough to kill over?"

"I don't know the amount, but when Rob was on the phone with the head detective, it sounded like it was a lot."

"Hmmm…do you know if they've talked to Courtney yet?" Gina asked.

"Yeah, they haven't. They needed to get some more information before they went to see her. I think they were going to go there later this afternoon."

"Then I need to get over to her place now," I said. "Just a friendly visit, and see if I can find out anything. Without telling her about the will, of course." I turned to my two friends and partners in crime. "Gina, you want to join me? Casey, I think you should stick close to Rob, and let us know if there's news, like if they're heading over to Courtney's, so we can get out of there before we're caught."

Casey sat up and brought her hands together as if she was going to clap then clearly realized how inappropriate that would be and stuffed them in her lap.

"Do either of you happen to know where she lives?" I asked.

"Yeah," Casey said. "She's in an apartment over on Lysander Avenue, but way down near the highway." She gave me the apartment number.

Gina and I left the warm, dry cafe, and set out in the drizzle to get my car. Hopefully we could beat the police to Courtney. Casey said she would call Rob and check in, before she left the Mustard Seed.

Worried about the time, I also asked Casey to call Laura

and Julie and see if they could come in earlier than scheduled and get the food started. I didn't want to have to cut short an informative conversation with Courtney.

Courtney's apartment complex was one of the few buildings in town that was built in the 1970's. The outskirts of Stratford did not have the charm of the rest of the town. A convenience store sat on the corner of the block, and a gas station sat opposite it. Litter had gathered along the edge of the juniper bushes that ran along one side of the store's parking lot. It looked like this neighborhood was the area that Stratford Upon Avondale had forgotten.

We climbed the wet, slippery outdoor stairs with the iron railings to the second floor. Gina led us to apartment twenty-three.

First we knocked. When that wasn't answered we rang the doorbell. Just as we were about to give up and leave, the door opened a crack. A woman about Courtney's age peered out through the narrow gap. She wore a bathrobe, last night's makeup was smeared under her eyes, and she had what could only be described as bed-head hair.

"Yeah?"

Gina said, "We were hoping to see Courtney. We're friends from the pub. Is she home?" Her tone was businesslike and lacked warmth. Snippy.

From the bristled look on the woman's face, I knew I probably should have been the first to speak. Gina's query wasn't the most welcoming. "No. Haven't seen her since last night," the woman said.

"Does that happen often?" I asked. "That she doesn't come home overnight?"

"Hey, I don't know you two, and I don't know what business it is of yours whether Courtney comes home or doesn't come home." She made a move to close the door.

Not wanting the door to be shut in our faces, I quickly said, "I understand. It's smart to be wary these days. We could be a couple of con artists for all you know. Or murderers." From the corner of my eye I could see Gina nodding.

Gina jumped in. "She's right. We could be, for all you know. But we aren't. We just have some news about a family member of hers and we're hoping to find her and pass along the message."

I eyed Gina, approvingly.

The door opened a few inches wider.

"Well," her roommate said as she stood surveying us to determine if we were serial killers or nice people from the pub. Pub must have won out, because she opened the door and told us to come in.

"I'm Maggie," I said, "and this is Gina."

"Anne Marie," she told us.

"Thanks for letting us in, Anne Marie. So, do you have any ideas where she might go if she weren't going to come home?"

"Normally I'd say her boyfriend's apartment. But since he's *dead* now, I guess that's probably not where she is." She clutched her bathrobe closed.

"Yeah, that is so sad, really awful," I said. Gina echoed me.

"It is, but to be honest I thought he was a slime ball. He didn't treat Courtney very well. Yes, he was pretty hot, but that wears off fast, you know, when they aren't so nice."

We both nodded in agreement.

Trying to steer the conversation, I said, "I heard a rumor that he was sleeping with that critic who got killed. That says slime ball to me!"

"Yes! Exactly! Courtney didn't know about it until about a week ago, and she went ballistic."

"God, I can't blame her. I sure would have," Gina said, crossing her arms over her chest and shifting her legs so one hip jutted out. It was a classic Gina stance.

"This news we have to give her, it sounds like it has something to do with that critic, Cressida. Did Courtney ever talk about her?" I asked.

"Oh, yeah. She hated her. Sounded like Cressida was always mad at her about something. I know Courtney had borrowed some money from her once, and I know she was trying to pay her back, but you know how it is. Money's tight. Even sharing this little apartment costs way too much. So anyway, Cressida would get mad when Courtney didn't have the money to pay her back."

Gina offered, "I wonder if this message has something to do with that money. Like maybe the family has decided to say, 'don't worry about the repayment.'" Well done, Gina. Keeping her on our side.

"That would be flippin' awesome for Courtney. I hope that's it."

"Did you see Courtney after her boyfriend died?" I was

careful to avoid using the words 'killed' or 'murdered'—they felt like there was an accusation they carried with them.

"She was here yesterday for awhile. Crying, mostly. Then, around three o'clock she just got up and said she'd be back later and left. Haven't seen her since."

Remembering to sound like friends of Courtney's and not investigators, I said, "Dang, that's weird. She didn't even take anything with her?"

Anne Marie shook her head.

"Well, Gina, I guess we'll just have to pass along the news that she's not around."

Turning to Ann Marie, I said, "If I give you my number, would you call me if she shows up? Then I can make sure the message gets passed along."

After we exchanged phone numbers Gina and I said our goodbyes and left. We walked back to the car silently, though I know we both were bursting at the seams wanting to talk about what we'd just heard.

Not until we were in the car did we dare say a word. Then we both started talking simultaneously.

"What if she—"I started.

"I think we should—"Gina said.

We stopped. Took deep breaths.

I asked Gina to share her thoughts first.

She snorted. "I forgot what I was going to say! But, I do think one thing. We're going to be in a whole load of trouble after the investigators get there and she tells them we were just there."

"Oh crap! I didn't even think of that. And here I went and gave her our real names." I hit the steering wheel. What a rookie mistake. "Argh, this could be a problem."

"Yeah. We need to think of a way to get out of it. But later. Right now let's discuss all that information we just got! Dang, that was a good call seeing her." Gina pulled down the visor to peer in the mirror and admire herself.

"Yes, indeed. Courtney's run. Why? Where to? And, most interesting of all was hearing how she owed Cressida money."

Gina added, "And remember you found that list of numbers in the guest book. Do you think she could have been adding up how much Courtney owed her?"

I thought for a minute. "Yes," I said without conviction. "But they weren't the kind of numbers that you'd think of as amounts a person would borrow. I would think they'd be numbers like 1,000, or 500. Or even 125. You know, round numbers. But not all of them were like that. I'm not sure, but I think one might have been 700, so that's a round number. But I know one was 1,137. Who borrows $1,137?"

"Interest? She might have been including interest."

"I suppose it could be," I agreed. Cressida didn't sound like the type to lend money without some compensation.

We arrived back at my apartment, and I rejoiced when I saw a spot right in front of the building. The earlier drizzle had turned to rain, and a short run into the house sounded much better than a block-long hike in that weather.

"Can you come in for a few minutes? We can finish talking it all through?"

"Sure."

Once inside, we peeled off our damp outer layers and I went into the kitchen to put the kettle on. A few minutes later I carried the teapot to the table and we sat down to steaming cups of fragrant tea.

"So maybe the numbers were money," I started. "And we know for sure that Courtney owed Cressida money. I'm fairly certain now that the argument Steve saw on Monday at the pub was about the money. Don't you think?"

"Oh yeah. I'd bet on it," Gina said.

"Why do you think she left town so suddenly?"

She finished taking her sip of tea before answering. "Duh. Because she had just killed two people?" Her upper lip pulled upward in a derisive snarl.

"That seems like the obvious answer. But if she did kill them, why wait a whole day before running away? Jeffrey died Friday evening, and she didn't get up and go until Saturday at three o'clock in the afternoon, according to Ann Marie."

"You know, we keep talking like it is for sure that Jeffrey was murdered. There still is a small chance it was an accident, remember?"

I picked up the thought from there. "If he wasn't a victim, would that change how we're looking at Courtney? I don't know about you, but at the moment my money is all on her as the murderer. But if Jeffrey's death was accidental, I'm not so sure about her having killed Cressida."

"I sure am!" Her sudden volume and enthusiasm startled me and my tea sloshed out of my cup. "Even if it was only Cressida who was murdered, *who* has a better motive for murder? One." Her right hand tapped the extended index finger on her left hand. "She owed Cressida money. Two. Cressida was always being nasty to her every time she was in town, probably on her case about the money. Three. Jeffrey, her boyfriend, was having sex with Cressida to keep her from writing any more bad reviews. Four. She's gone missing. One, two, three, four." She tapped the four extended fingers, one at a time. "I think it adds up," she concluded, flying her arms wide to further illustrate her point.

I stared at her and thought. Her case was clear and made sense.

"But now what?" I asked. "What do we do with this information?"

"I know we *should* tell Rob or the sheriff. But you know that since we already did that when we thought Jeffrey was the killer, they're just going to think we're crying wolf again. And they're gonna think we're getting involved where we shouldn't be," she said with a smirk.

I took a sip of tea, thinking. "Yes, and yes," I agreed after another sip. "I think for now we keep this to ourselves, and keep trying to find Courtney. Of course, as soon as they talk to Anne Marie, they'll be onto us." How we would handle that I had no idea, but decided to cross that bridge when we got to it.

I poured us each another cup.

"Any ideas how we're going to find Courtney?" Gina

asked, stirring an obscene amount of sugar into her tea.

"Maybe. I know we've gone to the well that is Steve too many times now. But what about asking some of the people she works with if they have any ideas where she could be?"

"I guess we could," she agreed without enthusiasm.

"You want to do the honors, and look into that, Watson?"

"Hey, who said you got to be Sherlock?" she argued.

"Would you be willing to be Watson if Mr. Benedict Cumberbatch was your Sherlock?" I teased.

She gave me a sardonic grin. Wagging a finger at me she said, "Well, duh! But honey, you're no Benedict Cumberbatch."

I laughed and snorted until the doorbell rang.

Pulling myself together I answered the door to a teary, miserable looking Casey. Without a word she fell into my arms.

"Casey? Hey, what's the matter? What happened?" I wrapped my arms around her, as I led her into the room.

She hiccupped and glanced over at Gina.

"I'm outta here," Gina said. "Whatever's going on, Casey, I hope things will be better soon." She put a hand on Casey's shoulder, then slipped out the door, quietly closing it behind her.

"Come sit down." I helped her to the couch.

Sitting down, she looked up at me, her eyes glistening with tears.

"No baby this month. Lucky thirteen. That's thirteen months we've been trying." The dam broke and the tears flowed down her face. I gathered her to me and held her tight.

"Oh, Casey, I'm so sorry. Damn."

She tried to say something but couldn't get it out. We held onto one another for a full minute before the sobs subsided and she pulled back.

"It's just so frustrating. But now we can see a fertility specialist. My doctor said we needed to try for a year before we should see the specialist."

"How's Rob been doing with it?"

"Not so well. He's sure it's him and feels like it makes him less of a man." She pulled a tissue out of a pocket and mopped up her face. "Of course, it's much more likely to be me, but I can't reason with him. I'm not looking forward to having to tell him about this latest failure."

Casey was always such a high-spirited, hyper person, that seeing this new serious, not to mention crestfallen, side of her was unnerving. My heart broke for her.

"You look cold, let me get you a blanket. Then I'll make you some tea and you can cry on my shoulder or yell and scream or do whatever you need to for as long as you want."

She spent the next hour getting it all out of her system, and I spent the hour trying to say the right, most encouraging things. By the end of the hour I saw a smile on her face and a hint of the optimistic Casey I knew and loved.

That was the Casey who would be needed to face the challenges that certainly faced her and Rob.

***

After getting Casey home and settled I was late to the tea room, which thankfully was in the capable hands of Laura and Julie, along with Gina's more rookie assistance. Julie wasn't able to stay, so Laura, Gina, and I worked the busy shop, never stopping to get a breath.

With a crowded room and each of us flying from tables to kitchen and back I barely registered the sound of the bell as yet another customer walked in halfway through the busy afternoon. It wasn't until I saw Gina nearly knock over a chair in her rush to greet the latest tea lover that I looked up and saw the remarkable personage of one Darius Thulani standing just inside the door. He filled the area.

Gina struck poses I recognized as part of her personal seduction repertoire, as she flirted with an enormous smile on her face. When she began to lead him to a table, I intercepted the two of them.

"Darius…hello."

"Hello, Maggie. Come to find out just how authentic your cream tea is," he said with a challenge that came off sounding more like a seduction.

With one hand on a hip, I lifted my brows and replied, "I'm quite confident you will find it just as delicious as any you could get in England."

"I don't know about that," he said, waving a hand up and down in front of me and then Gina. "Where's the classic tea room uniforms? With the little caps and everything? Don't know if I can trust a cup of tea coming from a woman without the proper English uniform." One corner of his mouth went up in a smirk that could have seduced most of the women in the room. And that probably was doing exactly that, as I could feel most of their eyes on us—or rather, on him.

As Gina pulled out a chair for Darius, I said, "I think you'll find that despite our lacking the proper attire, our tea is superior." Gina placed a menu in front of him, bending over farther than necessary to allow her to peer into his face one more time and give him her most toothy smile.

"Okay, let's see what you can do. I'll take a cream tea with a pot of Yorkshire Gold," he said without looking at the menu. "You *do* carry Yorkshire Gold, don't you?" he asked in his best Othello voice.

Lowering my chin and narrowing my eyes I answered, sounding a little piqued, "Of course we do."

"I'll get that for you, Darius," Gina oozed. She backed toward the kitchen, bumping into two tables on the way, never taking her eyes off Darius.

When the kitchen door closed behind her, I said, "You'll have to excuse Gina. She's a little star struck." Then under my breath I added, "Or something."

He looked up at me, his dark eyes on mine in a way that didn't allow me to look away. "What about the owner of this establishment?" he asked, his voice low to keep the people at the neighboring tables from hearing.

What was he asking? My background as a tea maker? My education? My political leanings? Or, my 'or something?'

"What about me?" I muttered.

The only answer I was given was another sexy smirk that knocked the air right out of my lungs.

"Um, Gina's new. I should probably get back there and make your tea myself." I shuffled gracelessly to the kitchen.

Once safely in the welcome refuge of the kitchen I collapsed on a stool.

"What is it about him that does that to a woman? Does he have more than his allotment of testosterone, or what?"

Gina stared at me like I was a slow child.

"Duh. One. He's gorgeous. Far too gorgeous to be safe. Two. That voice. Three. Those lips and the way they look when he smiles. Four. His—"

I put a hand up to stop her and said, "Yeah, yeah, yeah, I get it. It's just that he has an effect on me that is…unnerving."

I stood and pushed her away from the teapot into which she was about to haphazardly throw some loose leaf tea.

"I'll make the tea. You just make sure that there's a little extra clotted cream with his scones. And extra strawberry jam too."

"Ah, yes, nothing says 'I want you' like extra clotted cream," Gina said with a cackle.

Somehow, both Gina and I survived the next half hour with Darius in the room. In fact I believed we handled the situation very professionally. Each of us checked in on him, but left him to his tea and scones for the most part. At one point, an older woman wearing a floral dress and pearls cautiously approached his table and told him in a small, nervous voice how much she had loved his performance in *Othello*. I watched as he graciously thanked her with a warm smile. I'm sure she was set up for the rest of her day. Or week.

Just before he left I went over to him and asked, "Well? How was it? The tea up to your standards?"

He tipped his head to one side then to the other, and cocked a brow before answering. "Quite a good cuppa, Maggie. I'm pleasantly surprised. And the scones, too. Just like at home." He was giving me one of those looks again, and I shifted my weight back and forth from one foot to the other. I knew my face was reddening.

"I'm so pleased and hope you'll come back some time." I silently congratulated myself on how professional it sounded. I managed to keep all lust out of my voice.

He reached out and grabbed my hand. "If you promise to make my tea yourself, I surely will." He didn't let go of my hand, and I wasn't sure how much longer my legs were going to be able to keep me upright. Professionalism was in danger of flying on its way out the window.

"Of course," I eventually choked out.

There were several beats before he released my hand.

After he'd paid his bill and left far too much for a tip, he went to the door, but paused to turn. A slow, lazy smile became a wide grin and one eye winked flirtatiously.

When he was gone, the planets returned themselves to their usual positions, and the atmosphere in the room returned to normal. But I knew a few hearts were still beating at high speed.

~ nine ~

Sunday, May 24th

WHEN THE CLOCK CHIMED FIVE o'clock I was ready to drop into a little heap on the floor. Between the non-stop busyness of the room and Darius' visit I was knackered.

I shooed all three ladies out the door, while profusely thanking Laura and Julie for the emergency help. Only then did I allow myself to collapse into a chair, my head on the table.

I might have fallen asleep if not for the knock on the window. Sitting up I wearily looked in that direction. Once my eyes readjusted I saw Nate waving at me and mouthing what looked like, "Let me in."

Seeing Nate outside my window made some of the exhaustion dissipate, and I hurried over to the door with energy I didn't possess five minutes earlier. Despite all the fun flirtations with Darius, this was the man who made my heart swell.

"Hi, you," I greeted him, holding the door wide and ushering him in.

"Hi. You look beat," he said, examining my face.

"Long day." I ran a hand through my hair, self-conscious of what a disaster it had to be after being out in the rain several times during the day and working at a breakneck speed all afternoon.

"Then you need what I've come to offer. You want to grab a quiet dinner over at the Robin?"

I eyed him and wondered at the turn around.

He must have known what I was thinking. "I want to apologize for last night. I wasn't in a mood you would have wanted to be around. I thought it would be best to lock myself away and save society from my horrid attitude." It was impossible to say no to the impish crooked grin.

"It's okay. I know I've had a lot of days lately when I felt like hiding away. I'd love to have dinner with you." I looked into those green eyes with the golden flecks and the lips curved into the lazy smile and fought the desire to kiss him in a way he would never forget. Instead, I said, "Can I meet you there in about an hour? I have some clean up to do here and I'd really like to run home first and change into something that isn't sweaty, stinky, and stained with jam."

"I kind of like the jam stain," he said, eyeing the red splotch on my shirt.

I opened the door. "Sorry, it's not the look I try to go for. I'll see you about six, maybe a few minutes after."

"Good. Thanks. I'll see you there." He sounded like a bashful fifteen year old boy.

I watched him walk in the direction of his store before I rushed to take care of everything that had to be done immediately. The next day, Monday, we were closed so I could come back in the morning to deal with the rest of it. I needed every minute I could get before six o'clock to make myself presentable.

I wasn't striving for stunning. Presentable would do fine.

The romantic, dimly lit Robin, filled with well-mannered, soft spoken customers appealed to a different kind of diner than the more boisterous Garter. The decor was still authentic English pub, but somehow through the years the Robin had started to attract a more staid clientele, or those who wanted a quieter experience without spending the money that Tybalt's required.

Sundays, in true British fashion, meant Sunday Roast at the Robin Goodfellow. In England the meal was served at lunch, but to accommodate the tourists in town the roast wasn't limited to lunch service but instead continued into the dinner hours as well. The roast options included turkey, pork, and beef with all the trimmings. No one ever left the Robin hungry after a Sunday roast.

Nate and I were seated at a quiet corner table, lit with a flickering candle. Over a sumptuous meal of rare roast beef, golden roast potatoes, delightfully fat-laden Yorkshire pudding, rich gravy, crisp string beans, and tiny baby carrots we chatted companionably about everything except the one thing weighing most heavily on our minds. The murder investigation.

It wasn't until we were nearly finished and our bottle of wine almost empty, that Nate brought it up.

"I've heard there's another *person of interest*, but I was told I'm still a *person of interest* as well."

"Oh, Nate, I'm so sorry to hear that. Do you know who the other person is?" I asked innocently, as if I had no idea it was Courtney.

"No, just that it's someone who had ties to Cressida. One detective let it slip that it's a woman."

I peered into the depths of my red wine. "So. If I were to tell you that I think I know who it is, would that upset you?" I never took my eyes off the wine.

"Maggie…have you been up to your Miss Marple routine again?" He said it in a teasing tone rather than a frustrated one, giving me hope.

"Miss Marple? I thought it was Jessica Fletcher you didn't want me to impersonate."

My only answer was a cocked brow and a laser-like glare.

"Okay." I shrugged. "Well…maybe. Not really. But sometimes I just hear things. And Gina hears things. And sometimes Casey, too."

I looked up at him. "Do you want to know what I know, or not?"

His eyes traveled from my eyes to my mouth and back before he answered. "I suppose it wouldn't hurt," he said with a sigh.

"Courtney Parker. She's a waitress at the Garter."

"Yeah, I know Courtney. But she isn't a murderer, that's just ridiculous." He dismissed it as one would dismiss the reality of the Easter Bunny.

"I know. But it seems she's borrowed money from Cressida over the years and Cressida was getting angry about it not being paid back." I chose not to share the information about the will, and certainly not about Jeffrey.

"That sounds like a very thin thread to hang a murder suspicion on."

I laughed a short, angry laugh. "No more than the absurd basis for their suspicions of you."

Nate squirmed in his seat. Had more happened?

I ignored his sudden discomfort and took a sip of wine. Time to steer the conversation in another direction.

I reached across the table for his hand.

"You know, when this whole thing is behind us, we need to go out for a celebratory dinner someplace very romantic and make it through an evening without once using the words *murder* or *investigation*."

I was rewarded with a smile that made my toes curl. The candlelight played with the gold flecks in his eyes. My heart thrummed.

At least I thought it was my heart, until I discovered my phone vibrating in my purse.

I wanted to ignore it, but with everything going on I knew that wasn't an option.

"I'm so sorry, Nate." I rolled my eyes as I pulled the phone from my purse.

A text from Rob waited to be opened.

I clicked on it and read that he would be meeting me at my apartment at nine o'clock.

That couldn't be good.

"Jesus, Mary, and Joseph," I said, sounding for all the world like elderly Sister Josephine Rose at the convent. "It seems I have only twenty minutes before I have to meet Officer Rob Butler at my apartment."

"Any idea why?" The look on his face told me he was suspicious.

"No, none," I lied.

I had all too good an idea what Officer Butler wanted to see me about.

As Nate walked me home, he held my hand tightly in his own. When we arrived in front of the house, his hand squeezed mine almost to the point of pain. Rob stood on the sidewalk, in full uniform. By his side was a man in a suit and tie.

No this didn't look good.

"Rob," Nate said with a small nod.

Rob returned the nod. "Nate." He turned to me. "Maggie O'Flynn this is Detective David Petrovic."

Now it was my turn to squeeze Nate's hand until the bones began to break. He responded by resting his other hand on my shoulder.

Detective Petrovic looked to be in his forties. Not at all bad looking, he was tall, fit, sported a shaved head, was dressed impeccably, and had piercing blue eyes that made me want to confess to crimes I hadn't committed.

"You want me to come in with you?" Nate asked.

I wanted to shout Yes! But I didn't get the opportunity.

"I'm sorry, we need to speak to Miss O'Flynn privately," Detective Petrovic said. He didn't sound in the least bit sorry. His voice was free of any inflection.

I nodded, and released Nate's hand. Lying, yet again, I said, "It's okay. I'll be fine." I attempted a sorry excuse for a smile. So much for reassuring him.

With a hand on my back and the other one indicating the direction in which we needed to walk, Rob said, "Let's head on in, Maggie." I knew he was trying to sound friendly, but I also knew he needed to appear professional in the presence of the detective.

I shot one last look at Nate and said over my shoulder, "I'll call you later."

"I'll be waiting."

After we entered my apartment we sat down in my living room, Rob and I on the couch, and Detective Petrovic in the room's only armchair. He sat up ramrod straight.

Rob spoke first, clearly in charge of breaking the ice. "Maggie, we've found out about you and Gina visiting Courtney's roommate." He seemed to be trying to telegraph a message to me, one that said, 'sorry this is just my job.'

I answered with a nod, my eyes only on Rob.

"Miss O'Flynn, your visit to Miss Parker's apartment and the chat you had with her roommate could be seen as hindering our investigation. That's serious, and we don't take it lightly." Petrovic said. I forced myself to look at him and all I saw was condescension.

"So, what we're saying is you can't go off interviewing

people associated with this case," Rob clarified.

I said, to Rob, "I understand. You should know however, that I didn't know anything about Courtney being gone. I just…" I cut myself off before I said more than I needed to.

"Miss O'Flynn, we need you to tell us now that you fully understand the need to cooperate with us and not interfere with our investigation in any way. This could include talking to witnesses about the crime, talking to persons of interest about the crime, etcetera. Do you fully understand that?"

"Yes, but—"

"The only answer we are interested in, is 'yes,'" Petrovic said.

Surely he knew I was dating his prime suspect. I wasn't going to be forced to stop seeing Nate, was I?

As if he read my mind, Rob said, "Perhaps for the next day or two, it might be best to limit the time you spend with Nate."

Limit wasn't the same as eliminate, and I wasn't about to question it, despite the hackles I felt rising at the idea of such an order.

"Fine," was all I said.

"Miss O'Flynn," Petrovic started again. Obviously this was the only way he knew to start a sentence. "If we have to have this chat again it could result in you being detained."

What I had here was a clear case of Good Cop Bad Cop.

I gave him my new pat one-word answer. "Fine."

As if to make it all more official they each handed me their business card as they left.

I closed and locked the door behind them, went into the

kitchen and poured myself a large glass of red wine, and sat back down on the couch with my phone.

I took a deep swallow of wine as I hit Nate's number, not having a clue what I would or could tell him about my visit with the local gendarme.

And beyond the problem of limiting my Nate time, I had the little complication of how to continue investigating the murders without bringing on the wrath of Petrovic.

～ ten ～

Monday, May 25th

AS THE ONLY DAY OFF I allowed myself, Mondays were made for sleeping in. So when my cell phone started buzzing at eight, stirring me from deep sleep to foggy awareness, I briefly considered throwing it across the room. But then all of life's realities came rushing back to me and I blindly reached for it and answered the call.

"Yeah," I croaked into the phone.

"Is this Maggie?" a feminine voice asked.

"Yeah."

"This is Anne Marie, Courtney's roommate."

That made me sit up and rub the sleep from my eyes.

"Oh, hi Anne Marie. What's up?"

"Well, first the cops showed up yesterday afternoon. I told them what I told you, that I didn't know anything about where Courtney is. But I think I let it slip that you had been here already, and I'm really sorry I did that."

"Yep, they paid me a visit last night. But don't worry about it, you did what you had to do."

"Yeah, but that isn't the real reason I called you. Courtney called me this morning."

If I wasn't fully awake before, I was now.

"Oh! What did she say?"

"She said she just needed to get away. That with Jeffrey's death and everything else going on she wanted some space."

"Did she say where she is?"

"Yeah. She's staying with a friend in Westfalls." Westfalls is a small town about an hour's drive from Stratford Upon Avondale.

"Have you told the police about the call yet?" I feared either answer she could give me.

"No. Not yet. I wanted to let you know first. I mean you're a friend of hers and should know before they do. Right?"

I thought about that for a few beats before answering. "Right. Why don't you wait to tell them until later today." With each word I could feel myself writing my own arrest warrant. "But if they ask you directly, then I think you should tell them. Just maybe leave me out of it."

"Sure."

"Do you know this friend's name and where she lives?"

"It's Kate." She told me how to find her house.

I thanked her for calling me, reiterated the importance of answering direct questions from the police, and said good-bye.

Without putting the phone down I called Gina and filled

her in. We agreed to leave the house in a half an hour to set out for Westfalls and Courtney.

Westfalls is a pleasant small town that also sits on the banks of the Avondale River. A dramatic drop of the river, over massive rock formations, gave the town its name. The downtown is clustered along the riverfront. Kate's house was a few miles outside of the heart of town.

We pulled up in front of a neat, small one-level house. Spring flowers colored the beds surrounding the closely clipped lawn.

Our knock was answered immediately, as if we were anticipated and watched for. Courtney peeked out before opening the door wide and waving us in.

"Anne Marie just called. She told me you were coming over here. Can I get you some coffee?" she asked as she led us into the kitchen.

Gina and I quickly agreed to the much-needed caffeine fix.

After we settled in around the kitchen table Courtney said, "So, Anne Marie said you had a message for me."

"Yes. We do," I said. "There's news about Cressida's will. I think you're named in it." I hadn't originally planned to tell her about the will, but decided on the way over that the only way I was going to get any information from her was to give her something in return.

Before she could ask about it I quickly continued, "And you know the police are looking for you, right?"

She folded her arms and tipped her head to one side. "Yeah, and I don't understand why. Do you know?"

I looked to Gina, hoping she had an answer for that one. She said, "Not for sure, but we think maybe they're just looking for you because of the will. And well, maybe, and I really mean just *maybe...*" There was a lot of gesturing required to make her point. "...because you're named in the will it makes you, uh, a person of interest."

Courtney stiffened at that news.

"I didn't kill anyone," she spat.

Gina and I both did fake laughs that hopefully didn't sound fake. "Of course not. We know that," I reassured her. "You know how it is when they look at everyone who might have benefited from a death." I shrugged.

"Hmmm," she said.

"And I think I heard that they know you knew Cressida, from a long time ago," Gina shared.

Courtney nodded. "The miserable old bat. At least someone put everyone who knew her out of their misery."

So no love lost there.

"I only saw her a couple of times," I told her. "But both times she was an awful person."

"Oh yeah, that was Cressida," she said emphatically.

Treading carefully, I asked, "And Courtney, didn't you date Jeffrey?"

Her eyes glistened as she bit her lower lip.

She nodded, silently.

We sat quietly until she could continue.

"Turns out he was the creep everyone kept telling me he was."

"Gosh, I hope they don't think you had something to do with his death, too," I said, all innocence.

"Why would they?" she blurted. "If they're going to look at everyone who dated Jeffrey then they'd also suspect you, Gina." She waved her hand in Gina's direction.

My head snapped so quickly in Gina's direction a pain shot through my neck.

With wide eyes I stared at Gina, willing her to say something.

Staring at her coffee, she said, "It was only a couple times, and ages ago, like a year ago."

"Nice of you to share that with me. Watson," I snarled.

Courtney interjected, "Don't get mad at her. Jeffrey dated half the female population of Stratford. Thought he was hot stuff."

From what I had seen, he was pretty hot stuff. But of course, he knew it and used it to his advantage.

"So, if he was dating half the population," I started, thinking it through as I spoke, "can you think of anyone who didn't like the way he treated her enough for her to want to murder him?"

This elicited the first laugh to come from Courtney.

"I'm sure there were plenty of woman who would have been happy to see him dead. But I don't know who they would have been."

Courtney turned her eyes to Gina and let them rest there.

When Gina finally noticed, she jumped and throwing one hand over her heart, roared, "What?! You think I killed him? He wasn't worth the effort as far as I was concerned." She huffed and rolled her eyes.

Despite everything, I did take a few seconds to look at Gina and consider her as a murderer. No. A woman who dated a different man almost every week wouldn't have felt the need to bump off any of them. And she was *Gina*, my friend. My Watson.

"No, of course you didn't," I said confidently.

"Well, thank you!" she barked at me.

Unfortunately, there was still something niggling away in the back of my mind, though. Something that didn't fit with Gina and what she'd said about Jeffrey. I put it away for the time being.

"So, you said I was mentioned in the will," Courtney changed the subject.

Gina, still wounded, sat like a stone statue, so I answered. "Yes. And I think the only way to find out more about it will require you talking to the police. Might be better for you if you contact them before they contact you. They might be able to see you didn't kill anyone if you go to them."

Slowly nodding, she said, "Yeah, probably."

"But. And this is important. You can't say you know about the will. Just say, you heard they were looking for you. Explain you just needed to get away. And whatever you do, please don't mention that we were here and that we talked."

Courtney squinted at me. "Why?"

I scrambled for a logical reason. "Because if they think you're only talking to them because you want what's in the will, it'll make you look more suspicious. And if you mention us, then they'll put two and two together and know we told you about it."

I crossed my fingers she would buy that.

After what felt like an eternity, she agreed with my thinking.

We stood in the doorway saying our goodbyes when I quietly asked, "Courtney, did you know about Jeffrey having an affair with Cressida?"

Her face reddened and she snapped, "What?"

"Just something I've heard. Was it true?" I made every effort to use my gentle, nun-in-training voice that was supposed to make people feel comfortable so they could me everything weighing heavily on their hearts.

"I told you he was a creep," was her only answer.

I could see the lingering anger in her face.

It was time to let the detectives unravel the Courtney story and make a decision on whether or not she could be a killer.

Neither Gina nor I said anything for the first five minutes we were in the car. And when she finally broke the silence it wasn't what I was expecting.

"I'm starving. I need a big, fat, juicy burger. They make those around here?"

"Kind of early for a burger, don't you think?"

"It's never too early for a burger. It has all the important food groups."

"I think we passed a diner on our way in. I'll see if I can find it again. I'm hungry too."

"And disco fries. That's what I really need right now. Yep. Disco fries."

"Thought we'd ascertained that they couldn't be found out here in these Wild West parts."

Gina sulked, slouching in her seat. "No. They aren't."

Despite dying to ask her about the Jeffrey matter, I remained quiet until we pulled into the diner's parking lot and were shown to a table.

While Gina perused the plasticized menu, looking in vain for disco fries, I ventured, "So. Were you going to tell me about you and Jeffrey?"

Without looking up she said, "No. Didn't see how it was relevant."

"Hmmm," was all I said back.

The waitress appeared at our table and asked for our order. I asked for a cheese omelet and tea, knowing full well the tea would be tepid and undrinkable, and I'd be crabby about it.

When the waitress turned to her, Gina said, "I'll have the hamburger-pink in the middle. And a side of your steak fries. Then on those I want cheese sauce and chicken gravy."

Gina glared at the waitress, challenging her to question her order.

"I'm sorry," the waitress said coolly, "we don't make that, whatever it is."

Gina pointed at an item on the menu, "Says here you have baked potatoes, and one option for toppings is cheese sauce." She moved her finger to the next column. "And here you have chicken fried steak smothered in chicken gravy. So you have all the ingredients. I'm just asking you to combine them in a new and glorious way." She smiled disingenuously up at the waitress who stood slack jawed.

Through gritted teeth she finally told Gina, "I'll see what we can do. Anything to drink?"

"Root beer. Please."

When the less than happy waitress left the table, Gina told me, "I think I forgot to tell you the rest of the recipe for late night noshing. You have to have root beer with disco fries."

"I see."

Then it hit me. What had been bothering me in the back of my mind.

"Hey, Gina. So when we were watching Courtney and Jeffrey arguing that night why didn't you tell me you knew who he was?"

Our waitress returned with our drinks and placed them on the table with a sour, pinched look on her face. I touched the little metal pot filled with water. Not exactly tepid, but certainly not piping hot.

After she left, Gina took a sip of her root beer before answering. "You didn't give me a chance, Sherlock. You pulled that program out of your purse and you were all business finding out who he was. I wasn't going to steal your thunder." She smiled wryly and shook her head at me.

Gina had a talent of making even the most ludicrous things sound reasonable. For now I bought her story.

"I still think Courtney might be the killer," I said. "But, right now I'm leaning more toward Kristof. He still has all the right motive, means, and opportunity. For both murders. And he just makes my skin crawl."

"Crawling skin is recognized as murder evidence in

courtrooms the world over, you know," she cackled. "Maybe one of us should take one for the team and cozy up to him a bit and find out what we can," Gina said.

"You volunteering?"

"I would. But clearly he prefers redheads, not into hot-blooded Italian women. He was undressing you with his eyes at Tybalt's." She leered at me.

I shuddered. "I'll think about it."

The waitress appeared with arms laden with our order. She set my omelet down in front of me, "One cheese omelette." The burger was placed before Gina, "Burger, pink in the middle." When she sat the piece de resistance down she said, "And one order of whatever the heck you call this monstrosity."

"Disco fries. You might want to remember that name, because I'm seeing to it that this backwater state learns about the joys of good ol' Jersey disco fries."

"Okey dokey," she said as she left our table.

Gina gazed at the heaping pile of grease and fat with wonder in her eyes. I thought I saw a tear form.

"Oh baby, come to momma," she said as she dove in.

As it turned out, there was no need for me to go off stalking Kristof Lewis. I hadn't been home for more than an hour when my bell rang and I opened the door to a leering Kristof, bearing a bottle of champagne. At one-thirty in the afternoon.

"Kristof," I said through the partially opened door. I kept a foot behind it in case he had any ideas of pushing his way in.

"Maggie, my dear. Mondays. Love them, don't you? Theaters are dark, and I saw your little tea place was closed, so I thought we might enjoy some time together this afternoon." He lifted the bottle. "I brought the refreshments."

Everything in me was screaming for me to shut the door on him, but that wouldn't help me find out if he was a double murderer. Swallowing hard, I plastered a smile on my face and opened the door the rest of the way.

"I'll just get us a couple of champagne flutes. You make yourself comfortable in here in what passes for a living room." *But not too comfortable, please.*

As I returned with the glasses, I heard the cork pop. Setting the glasses on the coffee table I claimed the single chair in the room.

After he poured the two glasses, he sat down and patted the place next to him on the couch.

He held up a glass in my general direction. "Come on, Maggie, hard to get to know someone when they're halfway across the room." Each word dripped with the worst kind of slimy, macho seduction. Not only was it pathetic of him, but also sadly I guessed the routine worked on plenty of the women he'd tried it on.

"I'm quite comfortable right here," I smiled and reached for the glass. Once I had it, I took a sip to calm my nerves as they flared up around the despicable man.

He sneered at me, and took a sip.

"You know, Maggie, I think I know why you don't want to sit here next to me."

Ignoring him, I took a long swallow.

"I think you've decided I must be the murderer."

The tone of his voice made me shudder, and I squirmed in my seat to cover it up. That tone made me wonder if I had indeed let a murderer into my flat.

Gathering my courage, I asked, "Why would I think that?" I hoped it sounded casual enough.

"Oh, I know you were asking around at Tybalt's, about my whereabouts the night Cressida was killed. And I'm sure that visit to my office was a ruse to get information that would implicate me in the murder. What I don't know, however, is why you, a tea room owner, would be playing amateur sleuth, but it looks to me that that is exactly what you're doing." Malice oozed off each word, making the hairs on the back of my neck stand on end. "Are you, Maggie?"

"Hah, of course not. That's just ridiculous." I couldn't make eye contact with him and I knew he noticed it, giving him the upper hand. I tried, but couldn't.

"You sound frightened, Maggie," he said softly, measured. He drank half of his glass in one go and poured himself more.

I stood up and put my glass on the table. "I'm not frightened. But I think you should leave now."

"Oh now, we're just getting started. But we could get to know one another a lot better if you were here next to me."

"I don't think so." I was finished pretending to be polite.

He stood up, made his way around the coffee table and stood right next to me. Too close. I willed myself to stay put.

"You need to go. Now."

He reached out and took a curl of my hair between his

thumb and index finger. "I love your hair, and it's natural, isn't it?"

"Stop it!" I batted away his hand.

He laughed an unpleasant, unnatural laugh. "You *do* believe I'm a murderer! That's why you're so afraid and want me to leave, huh?" He leaned close to my face. Close enough that I could feel his breath. "Oh, but I had you pegged as a woman who liked a little danger. Why else would you be playing a sleuth? It turns you on, doesn't it?" He grabbed my shoulder, wrenched me to him and pressed his mouth to mine. I pushed back and jerked my head away, but he came at me again.

"No! Stop it!" I shoved him in the chest, with both hands.

"You're a little fighter. I like that." He kept moving toward me as I moved away, slowly making progress toward the door.

"Did Cressida fight back when you killed her?"

He made a sound that might have been meant to be a laugh. "Cressida again. You need to drop that. Not something for you to be involved in."

If that didn't sound like a guilty man, I didn't know what did. He lurched toward me, grabbed me with both hands, and pulled me close.

"You going to kill me, too?" I spat.

"Not if you start cooperating. You know, Maggie, you can't come on to a man and tease him the way you did the other night and not deliver the goods when he calls to collect."

"I certainly can." I lifted a knee and with all the force I could gather brought it up to his groin.

He shouted an expletive and doubled over.

I started pushing him to the door, as he moaned and cursed.

Once we were on the threshold I kicked him on the bottom, and he tumbled through the doorway. I slammed the door and double-locked it.

I heard him slump against the wall and groan while I went over to the coffee table, lifted the bottle to my mouth and drank deeply of the sparkling champagne.

Then I called Rob.

"But he didn't deny it. In fact he practically admitted it!" I tried to tell Rob, as I leaned far forward on my couch to emphasize what I was saying.

For forty-five minutes I had used my best debating skills to convince Rob and Detective Petrovic to take seriously the possibility that Kristof might be the killer. It soon became obvious, however, that Petrovic's debating skills trumped mine because he couldn't be swayed from his conviction that the man was innocent.

My frustration level was beginning to cause tears to press behind my eyes. Tears I refused to allow the two obstinate men to see.

Whether it was to placate me, or simply that they had had enough of me and my theories, Rob finally agreed to visit Kristof and question him again. Petrovic made it clear they would *not* be bringing him in for questioning, but that the meeting would be casual and at Kristof's own office.

Throughout their visit Rob sat in the armchair and Petrovic remained standing, arms crossed, brows knit. I addressed most of my comments to Rob.

After Rob's promise to talk to Kristof, Rob stood and Petrovic moved to the door, one hand on the handle. He couldn't get out of there fast enough.

Without enthusiasm I said, "Thank you for coming over and hearing me out. And Rob, when you see him, make sure you remind Kristof that sexually harassing women isn't okay either."

He gave me a wan smile and nodded. "Don't worry. We *will* take care of this, Maggie."

"Yeah," was all I could say.

Petrovic opened the door, then stopped in the threshold. He turned to me. "Oh, and Miss O'Flynn, you might be interested to hear that we've made an arrest. I think you know the man. Nate Larimer." He was out of the door faster than I had time to register what he had just said. Rob hung his head low and scooted out behind him, saying nothing to me.

My lungs felt as if someone had just punched them with all the power of a prize fighter. Try as I might, I couldn't get any air as my chest constricted.

Arrested.

Nate.

No.

That simply could not be.

No wonder Petrovic had no interest in anything I said about Kristof.

I stood at the open door, staring at nothing. When I finally could gasp in some air, I ran next door to Gina's and pounded on the door.

She opened it and nearly shouted, "What the...? No need to shake the whole house."

"Where have you been?" I asked, pushing my way inside.

"I had to go to the pharmacy for something for indigestion." She whined, resting both hands on her stomach. "I think maybe you have to be drunk to eat disco fries, something about the alcohol in your system must help them digest or something." A less than delicate burp escaped her throat.

Before she could continue on about her digestion problems, I said, "Gina! I texted you. I called you. And nothing from you!" While I'd waited for Rob and Petrovic I'd repeatedly tried to reach Gina.

"What's on fire?" she snarled.

"Uh, well, let's see. Kristof came over and tried to seduce me with champagne. When that didn't work he just went for it. He kept saying things that made it sound like he was practically confessing to killing Cressida and Jeffrey. I think he thought telling me that stuff was seductive." I shivered at the memory.

"Oh my god." Gina's face turned a deeper shade of nausea green.

Pacing up and down the room, I said, "It gets better. I called Rob. He and that Detective Petrovic came over and I told them everything that Kristof said and did. They don't believe that Kristof killed anyone. Or at least Petrovic, the idiot, doesn't think so. So they aren't bringing him in for questioning, but instead Rob will just go to Kristof's office and talk to him there."

"You're making me dizzy with all that pacing. And it isn't helping the queasy stuff. Sit down," she moaned.

"No. I haven't told you the worst of it." Glaring at Gina, as if she were the culprit, I said, "They've arrested Nate." Two tears made of anger, frustration, and worry escaped my eyes where they'd been pressing for the past several minutes. More followed.

With her raspy voice set to full volume, Gina barked, "Are you kidding me? No. Way. Just no."

"Oh yes. Yes indeed." I resumed my pacing.

"What are you going to do?"

"I'm not sure what I can do. I've pretty much done everything I can think of. And I'm more certain than ever that it was Kristof." I shook my head. "You have any more ideas, Watson?"

She pursed her lips and worked them back and forth, thinking.

"Nope. I can't think of anything."

"I think I'm going to go over to the bookshop and get whatever information I can from Frank or whoever else is there. They have to know something, even if it's just when they arrested him." At the word *arrested* my heart clenched up again.

"You want me to go over with you?"

"No, but if I text or call *please* answer!"

"I promise," she said crossing her heart with one hand.

"Go settle your disco fries damaged stomach," I said as I left.

Without any other workable options, I started praying for Nate. Maybe a higher power was what this situation required. I had certainly failed miserably.

～ eleven ～

WORD MUST HAVE GOTTEN OUT—the bookstore was packed, not with shoppers, but rather with curious people clustered in little groups sharing whatever information they thought they had about the shop owner. With heads bent toward one another, their furtive whispers filled the air.

Thankfully, Frank stood at the register. I waited as patiently as possible as he rang up a large stack of books for an older gentleman dressed like a 1950's college professor complete with elbow patches. This meant shifting my weight continuously from one leg to the other, taking out my phone every thirty seconds to check for messages, and occasionally twirling a long curl of hair around my finger and checking for split ends.

The customer asked several questions after Frank handed him his two bags of books. After the spate of queries, the gentleman regaled Frank with stories of his travels through

England. I repeatedly tried to catch Frank's eye, but failed. He actually seemed fascinated by what the man said.

I considered creating a distraction. Perhaps I could faint. Or have a seizure. Maybe I could pretend to hold up the place.

"Thank you, so nice chatting with you," the man said to Frank as he finally turned to leave the store. I took the two long steps to the counter and slapped both hands down on it.

"Frank!"

"Hello, Maggie." His tone was careful and neutral.

I leaned in, and lowered my voice. "What happened? Why did they arrest Nate?"

"Pretty awful, huh?" He sighed. "Rob and that detective came in about one-thirty or so and asked him to go outside with them. I followed them out there. The detective read him his rights, while Rob cuffed him. Nate asked them what had happened, and all they said was they would talk when they got to the sheriff's office."

"So they took him to Milford?"

"I assume that's where the sheriff's office is."

"How did he look?"

"Stunned. Surprised, you know. But he was quiet and just left with them like it was no big deal."

A woman carrying a small stack of children's Shakespeare books moved up behind me so I stepped aside and waited for the transaction to be complete. On the desk area several piles of books sat teetering. One was marked, '*to be reshelved.*' Impatient to continue talking to Frank, I picked up the top book and flipped through the pages for a diversion. It was an illustrated book of Shakespeare's comedies. As I mindlessly went through the pages, a small, folded piece of pink stationery fell out of the book.

I unfolded it and read the five words written inside.

"*With love, from your Troilus.*"

Clutching both the book and the note to my chest I stepped behind the counter and stood as close to Frank as I dared as he finished ringing up the woman's books.

When I was sure I would implode if they didn't finish up soon, Frank thanked her and turned to look at me with narrowed eyes. "What the heck, Maggie?"

In a rush of air, I said, "This book. It was on that pile there. The one that says for reshelving. Do you know who returned it?"

He looked at the cover. "Yeah, I sure do. That horrible Cressida woman. Practically threw it at me while she demanded a refund."

"Good. Okay." I chewed on my bottom lip while my heart pounded in my chest. "Do you have one of those books with the synopses of the different plays?"

"We should."

"Where?" I wanted to scream, 'Move it now, Frank!' but somehow contained myself.

"I'll show you," and he started walking, excruciatingly slowly, toward the Shakespeare section.

Running his finger over spines on one shelf he didn't find what he was looking for, and he repeated the process on the next shelf down.

Over his shoulder I scanned the titles on the spines, and had no more success than he was having.

"Wait. Here's one." He pulled it from the shelf, handed it to me and hurried back to the register where a customer waited.

Reminding myself to breathe, I flipped to the table of contents and found the title I needed. I turned to the indicated page, and skimmed the synopsis. Each paragraph increased my heartbeat, and I felt a film of sweat begin to form on my back.

With the synopsis book and the note clutched in my hand I ran up to Frank, and without stopping at the counter shouted, "I'll pay for this later. Call Rob and tell him to meet me at the Lady Grey B and B!" I was at the door and throwing it open when I added, "And Gina. Call her, too!"

It wasn't until I was cutting across the square that it occurred to me it was highly unlikely that Frank had Gina's number. But there was no time to turn back and give it to him. I started running toward the Lady Grey.

Out of breath after the sprint to the B and B, I opened the door and went in without bothering to knock. The heavy scent of potpourri assailed me. Looking into the front parlor I saw it was empty, and could hear the sound of a vacuum running somewhere upstairs.

Quietly, I tiptoed over to the door to Jane's office. It wasn't quite closed. I slowly pushed it open the rest of the way.

Jane sat at her computer, staring at the screen. Glowing on the screen, where I would have expected a spreadsheet or other document, I saw a picture of a scowling Cressida. It dissolved and another took its place. Also Cressida. Also scowling. If Jane realized I was there she didn't show it in any way, but continued to sit staring at the Cressida slideshow.

Softly, I said, "Jane."

She blinked several times in quick succession and lazily turned her head toward me. It took a few seconds before recognition showed in her eyes.

"Oh, Maggie. Hello."

"Hello, Jane. You have time for a chat?" I willed each word to come out sounding normal and calm, fighting the urge to stammer and scream.

"Of course. I always enjoy our visits." She stood, leaving the slideshow running, and shuffled out to the parlor.

"Can I get you some tea?"

"Not today. Not right now."

We sat down, Jane on the couch, me in the wingback chair that faced it. I sat on the very edge of the seat, my back rigid, hands still clasping the book and note.

"Jane, I was wondering if you could tell me a little about what you put in your basket for Cressida on this trip."

A look of confusion dissipated quickly, as she obviously warmed to the idea of talking about her favorite topic.

"Well, let's see. There was a box of her favorite tea, some tea biscuits, a pretty pen—purple ink of course," she chuckled about the ink, "a refrigerator magnet with

Shakespeare on it, a mug with a quote from Macbeth—the play she loved the most—and a book of Shakespeare's comedies. It was one of my loveliest baskets I'd ever made. She loved it, of course."

From what I'd read in the guest book, I knew she did not love it at all.

I nodded, trying to smile. "This note," I said, holding the paper unfolded and facing her, "you put it in the book, didn't you, Jane?"

She pressed her lips together until her mouth formed a fine, narrow line.

"Hmmm, I think so. Yes. How do you happen to have it?"

"Cressida returned the book to Friar's Book Shoppe. I picked it up days later and found this note inside."

I read the note aloud. "*With love, from your Troilus.*"

She lifted a brow and peered at me with a glint in her eye.

"Well, yes. A play on the words, you know. The play, Troilus and Cressida."

"Yes, I do know. In fact, I looked up the storyline while I was at the bookstore to refresh my memory. Troilus was the spurned lover of Cressida."

She crossed her legs, uncrossed them, looked at her fingers, pulled a thread that had come loose on her apron.

"Jane, were you in love with Cressida?" My body twitched with nerves. Articulating each word felt like a herculean task.

Jumping to her feet, she snapped, "Of course not!"

Willing myself to stay seated I adopted a casual tone.

"But I know you did care very much for her."

Clasping her hands in front of her, she said, "Yes. Of course I did."

"I think, in fact, you did love her." Before she could argue I hurried to add, "Perhaps *in love* isn't the right term, but you did love her dearly."

She collapsed back on the couch, tears welling up in the corners of her eyes. She nodded.

"I loved her for years," she moaned.

"And yet, she was so horrible to you."

"Not always," she cried.

"Really?" That was hard to believe.

"Not always. There were times when we would talk about things and she was nice. Kind even. It was just that she was so smart, much smarter than me, and I think she sometimes got frustrated with me and how dumb I am."

"But you aren't dumb, Jane."

She tilted her head and grimaced. "Oh, I don't know. Sometimes I think maybe I am."

We both sat silently. The large antique clock on the mantel ticktocked the seconds away.

"Jane, what happened? The night Cressida died?"

Shifting her eyes to the wall of pictures, she said, "I don't know."

"Yeah, that's what you said the first time we chatted. But here's the thing, Jane. I think you do know what happened. And I think you really want to tell someone about it. It's got to be just eating you alive, not being able to tell anyone. Maybe you should tell me."

She narrowed her eyes to mere slits and trained them on me. I shivered.

"Did Cressida hurt your feelings one time too many?"

Tick. Tock. Jane's eyes still bored into mine.

When she next spoke, the voice that came out of Jane wasn't her voice. Not the one I'd become familiar with. No, this voice was low, brusque, steely. "She laughed at me."

I gulped some air.

"Where were you when she laughed at you?"

Arms crossed tightly, legs crossed, head shaking back and forth, she said, "On the river path."

My heart sped up and felt like it would jump straight out of my chest. Where the hell was Rob?

Jane stood and crossed the room to the wall of pictures, and placed two fingers on a small rectangular blank area. By the shade of the wallpaper I could tell a picture had once hung there. Glancing over the wall, I noticed other newly vacant spots as well.

Finding it easier to talk to her without having to look her in the face, I sat with my back to her while she examined her pictures, and the spots where others no longer hung.

"What were you doing on the river path? Wasn't it pretty late?"

Her voice returned to the soft, childlike one I had heard on my previous visits to the Lady Grey. "Oh, yes. It was late. So late. I'd sat up there in that window for hours, waiting for her to come back." I *knew* the view from those back windows had to have something to do with the murder.

"Come back?" I knew I needed to keep her talking until

Rob arrived. And dang if he wasn't taking his sweet time.

"She used to go out late, usually meeting theater friends, people in the upper echelons of the festival, you know. She always came home along the path." A small giggle bubbled up. "Gave her a chance for a cigarette before she got back."

"Why were you waiting and watching for her that night?" I asked, getting more and more concerned that I was about to set her off.

I heard her take a couple of steps, probably moving on to the next set of pictures.

She took a deep breath and let it out slowly. "It was the night I decided to tell her how I felt."

"That you loved her?"

"Well…yes."

"What happened when you told her?"

It sounded like she was shifting things on the mantel as she considered my question.

"She called me a 'ridiculous old cow' and laughed." She spat the words out.

Throughout this interrogation, I had been looking down, mindlessly examining the design on the rug. For some reason right then I felt compelled to look out the window. But rather than seeing out to the trees what met my eye was the reflection of Jane with her arms stretched over her head, a large object held in her hands. She stood directly behind my chair.

I jumped up and leapt away from the chair, knocking my legs into the coffee table.

"Jane! Put that down!"

She continued to hold the heavy mantel clock over her head, but looked at me with foggy eyes. I didn't think it was me she was seeing at that moment.

"Come on, Jane. Put down the clock. You don't want anything to happen to it, it's so beautiful. An antique."

As a nun-in-training I had spent two weeks working on a suicide prevention line. We were taught, among other things, to use a calm, modulated tone when talking to those in crisis. Somehow, despite the fear I felt looking into Jane's desperate face, that training from years earlier kicked in, completely unbidden.

She blinked and gave her head a little shake. Slowly she lowered the clock.

"Why don't you sit down here," I indicated the chair I had just leapt out of, "and tell me how it must have felt when she said those horrible words to you."

Did Frank forget to call Rob? Good lord.

She lowered herself into the chair, and settled the clock on her lap, her arms wrapped around it.

In a quiet voice, she began, "It felt like she'd stabbed me. I had adored her for all those years. Took care of her during every visit. It was awful. So awful. I started to feel hot. So hot. Steamy hot." She fell quiet, her eyes staring ahead, unseeing.

"I can imagine." Soft, calm, modulated, empathetic.

"She said something about changing her mind and wanting one more drink, and turned around and started walking away from me. I told her she needed to get home and go to bed."

"Then what?"

"She yelled at me." I saw her arms tighten around the clock.

I waited for her to continue.

"She told me to stop acting like a nag. That I was just a fat, dumpy, stupid woman." She swallowed loudly. "That's when it happened. I didn't even think about it. I just picked up the biggest rock I could lift, and hit her with it. Right on the head."

The clock in her lap ticked noisily while we sat silent.

As I started to give up hope of ever hearing the rest of the story she muttered, "I didn't think I'd really hit her very hard, because she kind of kept walking for a couple of steps. Stumbling, you know. Toward the water though, not on the path. Then she tripped on something and fell facedown in the water. She didn't move. Just laid there."

Jane's face was a blank, her eyes staring at something, some *time* I couldn't see.

Shaking her head ever so slightly, she continued, "After that I don't remember much. The only thing I remember is hurling the rock as hard as I could into the river. Then I guess I just left. I remember being in my room and getting in bed with my clothes on. But nothing else. Until morning."

"I'm sorry Cressida was so awful to you." *Though maybe you could have thought of a better way to handle your hurt and disappointment. A way that didn't involve heaving heavy rocks at people's heads.*

She looked up at me, seemingly noticing my presence for the first time in several minutes.

"You're always so kind. So sweet, Maggie." *Then what was that with the clock?*

I worked at lifting the corners of my mouth into something resembling a smile.

"Do you remember the next day, when I came over to visit you?"

She nodded once, eyes again fixed on something in the distance.

"You were so genuinely saddened by Cressida's death. If you had killed her, why were you grieving so terribly?"

She turned her gaze on me, a look of confusion on her face.

"She was dead. Cressida was dead. However it had happened, I had lost someone I had cared very much about." Anger tinged her words and I glanced down at the clock, making sure she wasn't planning on raising it at me again.

"Of course you did. And I'm sure you felt some shock at what you had done, right?"

Jane scowled at me and shrugged. "I suppose."

Trying to affect a tone of nonchalance, I asked, "So Jeffrey. What was that all about?"

Her back went ramrod straight, and her knuckles whitened as her hands squeezed the sides of the clock.

"Jeffrey," she spat. "He didn't love her. But he was the one that got to be close to her." I saw her shiver. "How could she? How could he? I loved her."

"When did you find out about them?" It had been going on for years, so why did this upset her so much that week.

"I heard everyone talking about it at your tea room that

day. I couldn't believe it. First, Cressida hurt me before she died, then hurt me again beyond the grave." She moved to stand up, the heavy clock clenched tightly in her hands. "It was too much. Just too much."

Her face began turning a deep shade of red, while perspiration beaded up on her brow. I knew I was now in the wrong place at the wrong time if I wanted to continue on my merry way, unscathed.

As she lifted the clock, I turned and sprinted to the door, where I ran straight into Rob Butler.

He pushed me aside, went over to Jane and instructed her to put down the clock.

"Was just listening to your story, Ms. Morris. Very interesting stuff," he said as he pulled her hands behind her and clicked handcuffs into place.

I slumped down to the floor, listening to Rob read Jane Morris her rights.

I lifted the martini glass to my lips and tipped the last drops into my mouth. Dirty martini number three and I felt it. Probably not a bad idea to slow down a bit. Or stop for the night.

No, on second thought, I wasn't ready to stop yet.

Nate, freshly released from jail, Casey, Gina, and I sat at a table in the darkest, most out of the way corner of the Garter. It had taken me the first three martinis to tell most of the story about my time at the Lady Grey.

Yes, I needed one more for the wrap up.

After I got my drink at the bar—Steve had been very quick to fill my orders that evening—I stumbled back to the table ready to finish my tale.

"Okay, where was I?" I sat my drink on the table, not quite at the correct angle, making some of it spill over onto the tabletop.

Gina announced to all sitting within hearing distance, "Jane was jealous of Jeffrey."

"Oh yeah." I took a gulp of the drink. "So she actually orchestrated an opportunity to do him in." I pulled a finger across my throat and grimaced. "Jane got his number somehow and called him and told him she had something that she'd found in Cressida's room that she thought Cressida wanted him to have. She went into all this detail about how it was in a small sealed box with his name on it and she thought it might be something valuable. Then she told him she'd call back when it was a good time for her."

"She told all this to Rob?" Nate asked, incredulous.

"Yep. It was so weird. Like she was proud of how she'd figured out this way to lure Jeffrey and wanted to tell us all the details. Like to impress us or something. Sick. And spooky." I shuddered and took another swallow of the martini. I welcomed the warmth of the liquor as it spread throughout me. "She planned to meet him by the big boulder. The pest people had been spraying for mosquitos that afternoon, except they were finished down at that end of the path. She'd been watching them. But the barriers were still up, so she knew she'd have no interruptions—no one would see her killing him."

Casey made a sour face.

Nate pushed the basket of tater tots my way. I took the hint and paused in the story long enough to get a few into my stomach with the hope that they would soak up a little of the alcohol.

"Anyway, she called him when the coast was clear, and told him to hurry over and to meet her at the boulder. I guess he really wanted whatever he was imagining was in that box, because he showed up fast." I snapped my fingers. Or tried to snap them. I could hear my words beginning to slur and thought I might sound a little singsongy. I drank the last of the martini to help with my speech issues.

"When Jeffrey got there she just ran right at him and knocked him over so the back of his head went splat on the rock." I swung my arm in a large arc across my body, like a poorly executed upper cut and finished with a clap of my hands. Yes, indeed, that last bit of martini certainly helped. "All that was left was to drag him the half a foot or so to the water and put his face in it. She said she figured it worked for Cressida so it should work for Jeffrey."

"Well, she was right about that. It worked, all right," Gina said.

Nate waved the waitress over and quietly asked for a pot of coffee and one large mug. And another basket of tater tots.

"You know, what she really needs is a big ol' order of disco fries," Gina informed Nate with a wise nod of her head. "Sober her right up!"

Nate and Casey looked at Gina like she was speaking a language from another planet.

"Disco fries?" Casey muttered.

∽ twelve ∽

A week later

FROM THE DECK OF THE winery I could see miles across the valley. Situated at the top of a hill, the tasting room commanded a view of the vineyards covering the slopes of the hillside. The afternoon spring sun was warm, and I luxuriated in it. From the peaceful look on Nate's face, I guessed he was as well.

The week following Jane's arrest and Nate's release from jail was a jumble of almost daily interviews with the detectives as they tried to piece together what happened in both murders. When they finally told me on Friday they wouldn't need me anymore I almost kissed them.

Merry Wives Tea Room had its best week ever as Stratford residents and visitors alike heard the news of my encounter with the murderer and wanted to see me for themselves and get the story straight from the source. I'm afraid that by Thursday I was not as patient with retelling the story ad infinitum as I was earlier in the week.

Unfortunately, with everything going on, Nate and I had almost no time to see one another. Sitting on the deck at the winery it occurred to me that I still didn't know the entire story behind his arrest.

I plucked a few sweet grapes from the cluster on our fruit and cheese plate. After swallowing the last one I asked Nate, "So, you feel like sharing the rest of the story of your arrest? If not, that's okay. I understand. I've just been curious what made them decide, so wrongly, to arrest you."

He grimaced, and sighed before answering. "They got into her email account and found a couple of emails we had exchanged right before she arrived in town this year." After gazing into his glass of pinot noir, he continued, "She sent me an email basically trying to seduce me and convince me to be her latest amusement."

He eyed me before going on, as if to gauge my reaction. I nodded, encouraging him to continue.

"It made me sick, Maggie. It was disgusting. What she said. What she was suggesting. Just awful. I wrote back right away. I guess I should have waited until I'd cooled down and wasn't so angry before I replied, but I didn't. I told her in no uncertain terms to stay away from me, far away, or I'd…well, or I'd hurt her."

My face must have reflected my surprise because he hurried to say, "I know. I know. It was wrong to say that. And I hope you know I'd never hurt anyone, not even Cressida. But I wanted to make sure she got the message that I had no interest in what she was proposing."

I looked into those beautiful eyes of his, with the thick,

dark lashes framing them, and smiled encouragingly at him.

"I know you'd never hurt her or anyone. I'm just sad you had to spend even a minute in jail, let alone a day. But why didn't you go to the police with it, before they discovered it on their own?" I didn't want to sound accusatory, so I added, "You know what I mean. It always looks better when suspects divulge the information themselves."

He let out a long breath. "I knew I should have gone straight to Rob, or the detectives. But they already had me in their crosshairs and I didn't want to give them more ammunition. At least, not willingly."

"I guess I don't blame you."

I leaned over to Nate, who sat with his chair touching mine, also facing the hillside of grape vines, and gently placed one hand on the side of his face. As I leaned forward to kiss him, he took my hand and pulled it away from his face.

"Maggie, let's talk."

No good conversation in the history of humans has ever begun with those words.

I pulled back and peered at him through squinty eyes.

"I love our times together," he began, still holding my hand in his. "You're amazing. Fun. Gorgeous. Smart. Sexy." If he believed those things were true then why were we having this conversation? "But I think we should slow it down a little. These past weeks were…I guess the word would be *unpleasant*." He shook his head, and said "No. That's not right. Crappy. It was crappy. I want to get all of that out of our heads and just get to know one another better in a normal, murder-free sort of way." I could only stare at him.

Disappointed, I forced myself to say, "Okay. I guess I can live with that. But what harm would a kiss do?"

He laughed. My eyes widened—since when did kisses become amusing? Squeezing my hand, he said, "Well…in your books kisses quickly lead to other things." He lifted a brow, and in doing so looked rakish and sexy and my mind flew to other possible scenarios. The kind that might have been in my books.

"Nate, there's nothing wrong with those other things, you know."

"I know. But let's spend a couple of weeks getting to know one another better, under normal circumstances. You know, date!"

"I feel like there's more to this proposition of waiting." I peered at him, suspicious.

"Maggie O'Flynn." He shook his head, frustration showing. "Here's the thing. You used to be a nun and now you write what you call steamy romances. That's a lot for a man to just ignore and jump into bed with. I need some time to get to know the Maggie that's the real Maggie, not the one that has me a little intimidated."

I laughed. "Ah, there's the truth. I intimidate you." I laughed again before pulling myself together. "I don't think I've ever had that effect on anyone before. You know, I kind of like it." I sat up straighter. "Yeah, that's powerful."

He let go of my hand and gave my upper arm a playful shove.

My eyes rested on his before moving down to his lips that were pulled into a boyish, embarrassed grin. "Okay. We can properly date for a while. Actually that will be fun. But you should know I will be kissing you on these dates and that won't have to lead to anything else, unless you decide you're no longer intimidated by me and want more." I waggled my brows up and down.

He leaned to me, took my face in both his hands and kissed me. It was another one of those kisses that holds a promise of passion.

I resigned myself to the wait, knowing it could only make the fulfillment of the promise that much better.

It was hard to return to the demands of real life after the delightful afternoon with Nate at the winery. But I had asked Gina, Casey, Laura, and Julie to meet me at the tea room at five for a brief meeting. Always closed on Mondays, I felt uneasy asking for even a half an hour from them, but each had been gracious and agreed to meet.

Casey had asked if the two of us could meet a little before five—she said she needed a few minutes alone with me to tell me something. I prayed that whatever it was was good news, after last week's heartbreaking disappointment.

While I waited for Casey, I unpacked the three large boxes that contained the reason for the meeting. All alone in the room, I laughed aloud as I looked over the contents. Hopefully, the four women would be on board with the plan. I certainly expected some laughter at the proposition.

I threw a tablecloth over the items from the box just before Casey knocked on the front door.

"Hi!" I greeted her with a hug. "I really appreciate you coming in on a day off."

"No problem. And I needed to talk to you anyway," she said excitedly. When Casey got excited about something it was almost possible to see the electricity shooting off of her. Again, I thought of Sister Juliana and her supposed ability to see auras. Today, Casey's aura would have undoubtedly been brilliant.

"So, you going to keep me in suspense? Or are you going to share this exciting news?"

"Rob and I have our first appointment with the fertility doctor next week! I'm so relieved we finally get to start doing something positive toward starting our family. This doctor is supposed to be the best, and I sure hope he can help us."

I nearly jumped up and down with joy for her, but instead I pulled her into another hug. "I'm so happy to hear this, Casey. I know they'll be able to help you and you'll have that baby you and Rob so badly want. I have a really good feeling about this." And I did. I was sure that Casey would soon be a mother. A wonderful, loving, caring mother.

But for insurance I said, "I'll be praying for you two. Might even call a few of my old nun friends who have very powerful prayers and get them started, too." I smiled warmly at the beaming Casey.

Before we could celebrate any more, the rest of the crew arrived. After the requisite chitchat, everyone settled into a chair and I called the meeting to order.

"Ladies, for some time now I've been thinking about changing something here at the Merry Wives to make the place seem even more authentically English. Then, just recently, a customer mentioned the absence of the very thing I was thinking of adding to the place. I realize this is going to need some getting used to, and that maybe you might even laugh about it, or downright hate it. But I think—"

"Just get to the dang point," Gina interrupted, accompanied by a deep sigh.

I gave her a teasing glare. "As I was saying, I think you'll come to appreciate, if not love, the change."

I stepped over to where the pile covered with the tablecloth lay, and lifted the cloth. Before they arrived I had assembled one for an example.

I picked it up and held it in front of me. The simple black dress with the white Peter Pan collar fell to just below my knees. Over it was a white bib apron with ruffles at the shoulders, pleating on the bodice with four black buttons running down the front of the bodice, and a wide skirt, bordered with ruffles that matched the ones at the shoulders. Each woman gaped at me, mouths dropped open. But I still had the last bit to add. From inside the apron pocket where I had hidden it I took the little white cap with the ruffled edges and placed it on my head. I smiled widely at my audience.

"No. Freaking. Way." Gina barked.

Julie laughed. "You look like you just stepped out of a Dickens novel."

Casey stood up, hands on her hips. "Well, I like it! I think it's just perfect for the Merry Wives." She smiled broadly at me.

Laura spoke up. "I don't really care. If you're supplying uniforms it's just one less thing I have to worry about or spend money on."

Looking at each woman in turn, I said, "I think you'll get used to it and I'm pretty sure the customers will love them. It's the perfect touch to make this place as authentic as it can be. And Gina, I'm not sure why you care, since you're only here for a few more days."

"Yeah, about that, we need to talk," she said through gritted teeth.

Still holding my uniform up to my body, I narrowed my eyes and asked, "What is it, Gina?"

"Well, you see, that job I thought I was going to get? Yeah, well I didn't get it. Can I stay a little longer? There's this other one I know I'll get, but they aren't actually hiring for another couple weeks."

I was good at recognizing an opportunity when it was presented to me.

Draping the uniform over one arm, I said, "Yes, Gina, you may stay. Of course you may. However, there is one stipulation." I gave her my best gimlet eye as I paused for dramatic effect. "You have to wear this uniform, love it, and never utter a word of complaint against it. That work for you?"

She rolled her eyes, but said, "Yep. That works for me just fine. You'll never hear me whine or complain about looking like someone who plays a servant in one of your

British historical drama TV shows, or that I look like I stepped out of a Dickens book, or that—"

I held up a hand, palm facing her. "This right here counts too, my friend."

She fluttered her eyelashes and plastered a fake grin on her face.

After I adjusted the cap on my head, I held the uniform up against my body again, and did a few twirls and poses for my crew.

A figure moved past the window, then backtracked and peered in through the glass, taking in the scene before him. A wry smile played across the lips of Darius Thulani as he gave me two thumbs up.

I curtsied. He winked, and was gone.

Yes, the Merry Wives Tea Room was ready to move up to the next level of true Englishness.

And the quaint faux-English village of Stratford Upon Avondale was starting to feel more like home.

Though I could do without any more British murder mysteries.

On the other hand, there was something fun about playing the sleuth.

~ about the author ~

Monica Knightley is the author of mysteries, paranormal romances, and young adult novels. She makes her home in Portland, Oregon where the frequent rainy days are perfect for curling up with a good book and a hot cup of tea. When not fueling her reading addiction or writing her next book, Monica loves to travel with her husband—especially to England. A bit of England seems to make its way into most of her books.

You can follow Monica and find out about the latest additions to the *Stratford Upon Avondale* mystery series by visiting any of the following:

http://www.monicaknightley.com/

https://www.facebook.com/monicaknightleyauthor

https://twitter.com/monicaknightley

COME, BITTER POISON

COME, BITTER POISON, the second book in the STRATFORD UPON AVONDALE MYSTERIES is now available!

Sexy film star. Long-held secrets. Murder by poison.

When international stage and film star Miles Elliot comes to Stratford Upon Avondale to play Macbeth, Maggie O'Flynn is thrilled. He's been her actor crush for years. But when Miles ends up at the center of a murder investigation Maggie finds herself slipping back into the role of amateur sleuth. Before long many of her friends become suspects in not just one murder, but two. Maggie must discover who's poisoning people associated with the Shakespeare Festival before one of her friends gets slapped with a murder charge. And she must do so while dodging paparazzi that are stalking her because of a supposed love affair she's having with Miles Elliot.

With a bit of Shakespeare, copious amounts of tea, and a faux-English setting to rival anything the real England has to offer, *COME, BITTER POISON* is the second book in THE STRATFORD UPON AVONDALE mystery series. Lovers of cozy mysteries will find a cozy home in Stratford Upon Avondale.

Printed by Amazon Italia Logistica S.r.l.
Torrazza Piemonte (TO), Italy

12978876R00121